The Duke of Mamble's eyes narrowed on her. "Ah, it's you."

"Me?"

"Another woman who stares at a man with a title as if he's something to bite into."

"I would do no such thing," Gabby protested. "And you stared at me, too. It was quite rude of you."

"Is that so?"

"I was shocked by *your* boldness," she insisted. "A gentleman would not behave in such a way."

"Were you really surprised a man would stare at a beautiful woman? That's what you're here for. To be admired, and seduced. To turn a man's head." He looked her up and down, and then smiled at her in the very same way he had in the ballroom. He was almost undressing her with his eyes and clearly enjoying doing so. "You're a rather tasty morsel. I could be tempted to take a bite."

The characters and events portrayed in this book are fictitious. Any similarity to real persons, living or dead, is purely coincidental and not intended by the author.

HEATHER BOYD

MISS KIMBLE BITES BACK

Chapter One

"I heard Lord Brookes is sure to take a wife this year," Gabby Kimble whispered to Miss Daisy Ellis and Miss Justine Dawes as they stood together on the edge of the Earl and Countess of Windermere's grand London ballroom. "He is sure to attend tonight."

"I can't see him yet," Daisy complained but gave her an encouraging smile.

Lord Brookes was the viscount Gabby had already set her heart on marrying. Although it was still early in the season, she'd seen him riding through Hyde Park last week and had immediately appreciated the view. So dashing, so impressive on his russet-brown horse as it flew by, and surprisingly tipping his hat as he went by them. They had been introduced a few days ago, and she had become even more smitten with his attentiveness and good manners and conversation.

"I can't yet either, unfortunately." Gabby was not known to be led by her impulses, but she had decided Lord Brookes was the one who would capture her heart and hand in marriage. "I could ask our hostess where he might be?"

"Don't you dare do something so brazen," Justine hissed, apparently scandalized by her boldness. "A true lady waits for a gentleman to come to her."

"How can it hurt to ask?" Gabby shot back. "My cousin

seems willing to confide in me in just about everything else going on in society."

Gabby's cousin, their hostess Lady Windermere, was a very distant connection of her family's, and it had been a stroke of good fortune that she was willing to help with Gabby's first season. It made up for Lady Scarsdale, her older neighbor and would-be sponsor, returning to the countryside for her health, taking her son and new daughter-in-law with them. But she'd introduced her to as many as she could during the time she'd been with her and was humbled that she had enlisted her closest friends to help in her place.

Her cousin Bennett Kimble, her guardian until she was five and twenty years, had not felt it wise impose on so distant a relation. Yet that was exactly what everyone else did in society.

"I wish I had such a connection to share gossip with me," Miss Ellis confessed, casting her eyes behind them to where their guardian's stood. Irritation flashed in her eyes momentarily before a smile reappeared.

Miss Ellis was here because *her* guardian, a stern viscount, did his duty to his ward and had brought her out this year, but followed her everywhere. Miss Ellis had no mother or father too, or a wealthy cousin well placed in society to offer support during this difficult time.

But Miss Justine Dawes had been brought out by her older widowed sister, a woman who had triumphed in her own first season and snared a great matrimonial prize to become a viscountess.

Gabby wished to do as well.

Her season was beyond anything she'd ever imagined so far. It would only get better, too.

Her cousin Lady Windermere had excellent taste in friends, right down to the husband she had married. Lord Windermere was a handsome devil, wealthy, and with a generous spirit toward so distant a relation of his wife's. Gabby was beyond grateful, yet there was only so much they could do to secure her a husband. The rest was up to Gabby. She was intent on making a good impression on the right gentleman as fast as possible.

She smoothed her skirts and refreshed the smile on her face. She wanted everyone to believe she belonged here. "I hope I can speak with him tonight. He was so polite and kind when I ran into him on Bond Street yesterday," she murmured, and then caught Justine's frown of disapproval for mentioning the man again. "I swear I did not run into him on purpose."

It *had* been an accident, their collision. A fortunate accident. Serendipity, indeed. She'd been walking along, chatting with her cousin Bennett, when a scamp of about ten years old rushed past her, knocking her off balance. Gabby had stumbled straight into Lord Brookes' path.

And he'd caught her!

Right there on the street.

Gabby had been in a viscount's arms for mere seconds, but she recalled every exquisite moment as if it were a whole hour. Surely there was no better sensation than being held close by an attractive man!

"Well, I'm glad he caught you, so you were not hurt yesterday," Daisy whispered. "But you should not read too much into such a moment."

"No, she certainly should not," Justine agreed, "You know nothing about him."

"I know I shouldn't, but I have made discreet enquiries." She rattled off a list of his interests and achievements to her friends. Information she'd gleaned from conversation with Lady Windermere. "Is that not further proof that he's a fine gentleman and worthy of our regard?"

Daisy giggled. "You mean *your* regard. Justine and I have not the same interest in that particular gentleman as you seem to do. I'll keep an open mind about my prospects for finding a husband this season, as will Justine, I suspect."

"Yes, indeed," Justine agreed, but then frowned. "My decision regarding a husband will be well-considered and not the result of girlish speculation. I shall not be disappointed."

Despite the rebuke from Justine, Gabby linked arms with her friends. "None of us will. This is our year. We're *all* going to marry well and stay good friends forever, aren't we?" she asked, knowing the answer already.

Gabby, Daisy, and Justine were an unstoppable team. The best of friends, despite only having just met. They could help each other navigate society this season. They'd met at their first ball, stood on the sidelines together as others danced. They had struck up a hesitant, whispered conversation since they had not yet been introduced to each other. After the formalities were performed, there had been nothing to stop their merry chatter every time they met.

"Now, do you think we've stood here too long? Let's not be accused of being wallflowers and setting down roots. I think there might be a better view of the room from closer to the refreshment table." Gabby glanced over her shoulder to where her cousin Bennett stood talking with Daisy's guardian, Lord Throsby, and gave him a subtle, prearranged signal they would circulate. Bennett inclined his head, ready to shadow her everywhere.

They skirted the dance floor, weaving through guests not currently participating in the dance, until they found a suitably sized gap in the crowd on the other side of the room.

"This is much better," Gabby announced, fluffing out the skirts of her finest satin ball gown. They had a fine view of the dancers, anyone at the refreshment table, and also the ballroom doors, where guests flowed through constantly.

"I still cannot see anyone new, or *your* lord," Daisy whispered. Like Gabby, she too was hoping to make a good match this season but was willing to sacrifice her time to help Gabby with her singular pursuit of Lord Brookes' favor first.

Gabby rose on her toes slightly, and then back down when she spotted their hostess headed their way. She was desperate to make a continued good impression on Lady Windermere. She was a countess of remarkable influence in the *ton*, both before and after she'd married her earl.

But she was also lovely and kind and had wished Gabby success in her first season. She didn't have to feign her delight when the woman stopped in front of them and smiled warmly. Gabby dipped a low curtsy and rose. They had already spoken once at the door. "It is a wonderful evening, my lady."

"Thank you, my dear, and may I say again how lovely you look tonight." She smiled and glanced to each side of her. "You all look lovely."

"Thank you," they all murmured, the other two blushing a pretty shade of pink.

Gabby lowered her voice. "I took your advice to call on

the bookseller you recommended this morning. Such a collection to choose from. Bennett was in raptures."

"And yourself?"

She nodded quickly. "I found many a volume to please me, too."

Gabby was not sure she should announce to the world how much of a bluestocking she already was. Prospective husbands were said not to like women who might exceed them in education. But since coming to live with her older cousin, she'd devoured every book in his collection and now had to wait until he added more when funds and fate permitted.

"A woman can never acquire too much knowledge of the world," Lady Windermere told them all, before something caught her eye. "Oh, how wonderful. He came. Do excuse me, ladies. There is someone I must speak to," she whispered and then rushed off, calling out, "Sebastian!"

They all swiveled to watch the woman greet an exceedingly handsome stranger with great enthusiasm. Someone Gabby had never seen before, but from whom she could not look away. The man had a *presence* she'd not encountered before. She straightened her spine as her cheeks grew strangely hot just looking at him from this distance.

Gabby cleared her throat. "Do we know who that is?"

Justine leaned close. "That is Sebastian Spence, the Duke of Mamble. They say he keeps his older sister imprisoned."

Gabby gaped. "Who says that?"

"Well, everyone worth knowing in higher society," Justine murmured. "My sister was speaking of him just the other day. She's shocked he's dared show his face in Town."

The Duke of Mamble was a truly wicked man then. But this was the first gossip Gabby had ever heard of him. "He doesn't look wicked," she whispered, noticing a thousand things about him at once. Tall but not too tall, broad in the chest and strong-muscled legs encased in evening breeches. His clothing was first rate, but his golden-blond hair was a little long to be considered fashionable. He had the look of a man used to getting his own way. That was the nature of dukes, though.

Justine nudged her. "Looks can be deceiving. He banished his other sister to the countryside, too. My sister hasn't seen her in years and years, and they were once very close."

"I can't believe anyone would talk to him if that were true," Daisy whispered, eyes narrowed with suspicion, both on the duke and on Justine. "And why would Lady Windermere invite such a creature to her ball if it were true?"

"I've no idea," Justine whispered. "My sister told me to stay far away from him and I intend to. Maybe she *had* to invite him for some reason."

Gabby glanced at her cousin, Bennett, wishing he might be standing closer to hear these rumors and voice his opinion. He'd visited London before and seemed to know a surprising number of fellows in society. Bennett would not want her around a bad man and Lady Windermere might try to introduce her, as she had with many eligible bachelors so far.

Until she knew the truth of how to behave around the duke, she decided she must ignore his appeal, but once she peeked in his direction again, she could not seem to look away.

He didn't look cruel, but as Justine warned, first impressions were not always accurate.

He was more handsome than anyone else in the room, though, and he had such a presence that she remained aware of him even when not looking in his direction. He'd a serious face, a straight nose, but his full lips drew her eye as he conversed. He did not smile with the same zeal Lord Brookes shared with everyone he met, but he was mesmerizing just the same.

Mamble's dark gaze flickered restlessly about the room even as he conducted a prolonged conversation with Lady Windermere. It was clear they were well known to each other, and friends, which seemed absurd, given the rumors about his cruel behavior toward his sisters.

His eyes passed over her position quickly—but then they returned to her and her friends.

The warmth she'd felt upon studying him intensified as their eyes met and held across the crowded room. His eyes narrowed and Gabby could feel a blush climbing her cheeks with his prolonged scrutiny. It was almost impolite the way he stared at her, but she held her ground as long as she could, refusing to be intimidated by a powerful man so far above her.

Eventually, the corner of his mouth quirked up in amusement and he looked back at Lady Windermere, resuming his conversation with her as if Gabby was already forgotten.

Gabby dragged her eyes away from him and finally found Lord Brookes and his sunny smile directly across the room from her. She let out a sigh of relief to see the viscount at last. She was already halfway in love with the man and had no need to look at the figure of so notorious a duke.

Gabby whispered to Daisy, "Let's move again."

"But we just got here," Justine complained. "Oh, has Lord Brookes arrived?"

"Yes, indeed he has," she reassured them, ignoring the flutter in her stomach from nerves, "and not a moment too soon."

Lord Brookes looked so handsome tonight and, as ever, he chatted with a large group of ladies that surrounded him. The man she had set her heart on marrying was already laughing and clearly enjoying the attention he was receiving from those nearby. She desperately wanted to be one of them.

She wanted to be the most important one of all to him, too, but she could not butt into his conversation. She had to wait for him to come to her as Justine claimed.

Daisy nudged her. "I wonder why Brookes was so late arriving?"

Gabby turned to Daisy. "I do not know, but he's here now and clearly in a good mood."

"Whenever is he not?" Daisy asked dryly. Daisy had a deep suspicion of gentlemen who smiled too much. She thought them all disingenuous.

Gabby smiled a lot herself, hiding her discomfort as she fidgeted with her empty dance card. Lord Brookes was known to be fond of dancing and always in good humor. They were the things she liked about him most of all. Some men could be moody creatures. Her cousin Bennett was a prime example of that. Unhappy on occasion but often unable to say why. There was little she could do to lift him from his black moods, and she was always glad when he took himself away on days like that.

Gabby straightened her spine and hoped to make herself even more appealing and earn a dance partner. The right one would be Lord Brookes, but he hadn't noticed her yet. "Let's go around to the left a bit farther, so he sees us standing together."

They tried, but a set was ending, and the guests filed dutifully off the dance floor to rejoin their own parties, slowing their progress.

She fought the tide to remain beside Daisy but soon realized that Justine had somehow fallen behind. The current was too strong to turn back to fetch her and propelled her to the edge of the room instead. She held firm to Daisy's elbow as they found an open space near a window. When she rose on her tiptoes, she spotted the feathers Justine wore on her head, quite some distance away. She had returned to her sister without saying goodbye.

"Well!"

"Well, indeed," Daisy agreed, frantically fanning her face. But then she leaned close. "I swear someone just caressed my bottom."

Gabby snapped out her fan, too, but only to speak behind. "Really?"

Daisy nodded. "Say nothing to my guardian about it. He'll only become cross if he learns such a thing occurred right under his nose."

"Agreed."

Lord Throsby was unnaturally strict and protective of Daisy. She endured all sorts of ridiculous rules about where she could go and who she was permitted to talk with. Gabby suspected she had only just passed muster herself. "I would never break a confidence to your guardian," she promised.

"Nor I," Daisy whispered back.

Their guardians drew close, forming a protective wall to save them from being jostled about again.

Daisy suddenly pressed the back of her hand to her brow. "Lord Throsby, would you mind fetching us a glass of punch each?"

Lord Throsby, a man not inclined to take orders well, glared at Daisy and then Gabby, and finally grunted, "Stay with Kimble."

Lord Throsby did not like to have Daisy out of his sight for long or left to her own devices. It was a miracle he trusted Bennett with the task of watching over her. Throsby's behavior might have been endearing if the man possessed a little gentleness in his soul. But they were ward and guardian only, argued constantly behind closed doors, and had nothing in common, or so Daisy claimed.

Bennett was a much better guardian. He did not want to be privy to every conversation Gabby ever had. He trusted her not to make a fool of herself and gave her space to make her own mistakes. When Bennett wandered away to admire a nearby painting and gave them privacy to talk, Daisy sighed heavily. "I wish Lord Throsby would do that."

"Bennett has no interest in eavesdropping on our conversation," Gabby assured her. "Unlike your guardian."

"Lord Throsby wants to hear absolutely every word I say. Yesterday he asked what I ate when we were apart, and once, some time ago, what I dreamed of at night. I could never tell him that," Daisy whispered, a blush climbing her cheeks. "It would be just the excuse he needs to haul me back to the countryside and lock me in my chambers until I reach my majority."

Gabby squeezed her friend's hand. "Not long now."

"Yes. When my twentieth birthday comes, I will finally be free of him," Daisy murmured. "I will never understand why my father made him my keeper, but I am glad he did not extend the guardianship until I was five and twenty."

"Well, Throsby is a stick in the mud but at least you have no fear he'd take advantage of his position and misappropriate your funds," Gabby whispered. Lord Throsby was obscenely rich in his own right and astute in his business dealings.

"Because there's nothing much of mine to spend unwisely," Daisy replied, a little sadly. "I suppose I should be grateful he's willing to foot the bill for my entire season."

"He might be a little stern, but for you, he's a generous man," Gabby suggested.

Daisy scowled. "A *little* stern?"

"Well, maybe that isn't quite the right description for him."

"No, it is not," Daisy promised. "I swear, sometimes the way he looks at me, he's considering putting me over his knee because I disagree with him," Daisy announced, her face turning an even brighter shade of pink.

Gabby was shocked. "Has he ever done so?"

"No. But I'm sure that time I went shopping alone with you without telling him where I was going sorely tried his patience."

Gabby laughed. "You were not unprotected."

"To his mind, debutants do not make adequate

chaperones for each other," Daisy said, laughing merrily. "If not for your cousin Bennett claiming we had a servant watching over us, he might have forbidden me from your friendship entirely."

Gabby glanced at Bennett, filled with gratitude for his deception and support. Bennett and Throsby had become close in recent weeks, and it had helped strengthen her friendship with Daisy. "I have long suspected our guardians have made a pact."

Daisy's eyes widened in alarm. "What sort of pact?"

"To keep you wild pair out of trouble," Bennett murmured, laughing, as he suddenly rejoined them. "Stow your complaints away for later, ladies. Throsby returns and he's easily made suspicious by your laughter."

When Lord Throsby joined them, frowning still, and had passed her and Daisy a drink, Bennett said nothing of Daisy's complaints but did engage in conversation with the man to distract him.

Gabby smiled to herself. Her cousin was the best friend she had ever had. Loyal and not at all severe like Throsby. She couldn't imagine living with *that* viscount as her shadow. He'd no sense of humor or sense of adventure.

When their glasses were empty, they returned to the edges of the dance floor and then Bennett asked Daisy to dance with him.

Lord Throsby gave Daisy a nod of permission to accept before she answered Bennett's invitation.

Bennett swept Daisy away to the dance floor, leaving Gabby standing with the glowering Lord Throsby on the sidelines. Gabby shuffled her feet, unhappy with this turn of events. Not once had Lord Throsby ever asked Gabby to dance. He insisted he was there to watch over his ward, Daisy, and not engage in frivolous nonsense.

She looked around for Justine to save her but found her dancing, as well.

Gabby tried not to sigh with disappointment at being left on the sidelines. She had no hope Lord Throsby would offer to partner her tonight, or introduce her to someone who might, so she begged to be excused to visit the retiring room.

"Up the stairs and to the right," Throsby informed her as he took out his timepiece. "You have five minutes to return."

She struggled not to roll her eyes. Daisy had mentioned before that Lord Throsby timed absolutely everything she did. Five minutes was hardly long enough if other ladies were using the facilities ahead of her, but she did not bother to argue with the viscount and took herself off alone, fully intending to take the amount of time she needed.

Bennett was never so strict about her movements or punctuality, and for that she was profoundly grateful.

The Windermere London home was vast. While it might have intimidated her at first, she'd quickly grown used to such opulence. Yet she still glanced upward at the elaborate plasterwork ceiling and marveled at the effort it must have taken the craftsmen to complete.

As she lowered her gaze, she spotted a figure disappear into the library. Gabby was convinced it was Lord Brookes, and she debated the wisdom of following to find out for only a moment. If she could catch the viscount in the library, he might ask her to dance.

Gabby squared her shoulders, headed for the library doors, but she did check over her shoulder first to make sure

Lord Brookes had not followed. No one was nearby, not a guest or even a servant and she slipped inside unseen.

Gabby spotted Lord Brookes, already sitting in a high-backed armchair with his back to the door and facing the fireplace. She could just see the top of his uncovered head and the candlelight illuminated his hair until it glowed gold.

Gabby moved toward him. "My lord," she whispered.

"Leave it and go," he drawled.

Gabby was not to be deterred by his abrupt tone. "I'm not a maid, my lord, but someone who wishes to say how ardently I admire you."

His head turned slightly. "Really?"

"Indeed." Gabby gulped and decided there was no point in hiding the truth. He was alone, and she was being bold, but it was too late to turn back now. "My lord, I wish to tell you that from the first we met, I have longed to know you better than anyone could."

There was silence for a long moment, and then he stood and turned.

Gabby's mouth fell open, and she covered her lips as she whispered in horror, "You're not Lord Brookes."

"And there are a thousand reasons why I am grateful to be spared that fate," the unsmiling Duke of Mamble said, and then his eyes narrowed at her. "Ah, it's you."

"Me?"

"Another woman who stares at a man with a title as if he's something to bite into."

"I would do no such thing," she said, affronted. "And you stared at me, too. It was quite rude of you."

He drew closer, a smile twisting up his lips. "Is that so?"

"I was shocked by *your* boldness," she insisted. "A gentleman would not behave in such a way."

"Were you really surprised a man would stare at a beautiful woman? That's what you're here for. To be admired, and seduced. To turn a man's head." He looked her up and down, and then smiled at her in the very same way he had in the ballroom. He was almost undressing her with his eyes and clearly enjoying doing so. His gaze lingered on her lips and then dipped lower. "You're a rather tasty morsel. I could be tempted to take a bite."

Gabby's face grew hot, as did the rest of her under such intense scrutiny. She could imagine...no, she shook her head. She really shouldn't imagine his mouth anywhere near her skin!

But since no one had ever spoken to her this way before, she wasn't prepared for such an encounter. The duke was outrageously bold, and he knew his words affected her. There was no doubting the depravity of his thoughts as he regarded her, and probably every other woman he'd ever met. Yet she had no fear of him. "You should not say such things to a lady."

"Why not? It saves time," he said, shrugging away her rebuke. "Besides, I doubt you're *truly* shocked by me. If you were, you would have run to hide behind your mama's skirts by now. Or were you hoping to be compromised and become my duchess now?"

Now that was too much of an insult. She glared up at him. "I do not desire or deserve such an elevation, but you don't scare me, either."

"Don't I?" He stepped closer, his eyes searching hers. "You're trembling."

"No, I'm not," she insisted. However, that was not true. She was irritated by him and his groundless assumptions.

"Yes, you are. You came here looking for Brookes, but now linger with me. You say you're a proper lady but here you still are. I think you like to live dangerously."

"How dare you? You don't know me, and you have certainly formed a wrong opinion of my character," she seethed. She would have continued to give him a piece of her mind, but his finger was suddenly pressed firmly over her lips.

No man had ever touched her face, let alone her lips. Lord Mamble's finger was warm and, before she knew it, her tongue darted out to touch that digit of his, or perhaps push it away.

His eyes flared, and a wicked smile curved his lips. "Not proper at all," he whispered as his finger dragged slowly off her bottom lip and then, to her shock, he circled around to stand at her back. "I like that in a woman."

"I did not come here for you."

He moved around to face her again and bent until their eyes were on the same level. Gabby's heart raced as she stared into the duke's eyes. Blue, like the sea after a storm. A woman could become lost in his gaze if she let herself.

Gabby glanced down as her knees trembled.

The duke drew closer still and she could almost feel his cheek against hers, his breath across her ears. Hers caught, dreading, expecting his next move to be an attempt to steal a kiss. Her breath came too fast while she waited.

"What a shame you're an innocent." He drew back. "Run away now, kitten. Come and see me when you've more experience of the world."

Gabby looked up at him slowly. She did not appreciate being dismissed like she was a mere child.

Mamble suddenly grabbed her by the shoulders, spun her about on the spot, and gave her backside a hard slap that sent her stumbling toward the door even as it burst open.

Lady Windermere stood there for a moment, and then her gaze lifted past Gabby to the duke. Her eyes took them both in, together, alone in a room distant from her ballroom, and she narrowed them dangerously on the duke.

Mamble laughed. "Herd her back to your little flock, Esme. This one's not ready for a wolf like me."

Gabby hurried toward Lady Windermere even before being beckoned. "Are you all right?"

"Yes." She did not want Lady Windermere to think she had been compromised. "Nothing happened," she promised. Lady Windermere nodded and ushered her from the room. As she fled back to the ballroom, she struggled to know what to think of that encounter. She was unnerved by her narrow escape but also confused that she'd stayed. Would she have done so had the viscount been flirting with her that way instead?

Chapter Two

"WOULD it hurt you to be nice to at least one debutant this season?" Esme, Lady Windermere, chided, after a prolonged silence of several minutes following the young lady's departure from the library.

"If I had good reason, I might consider it," he assured her, sitting down again and crossing one leg over the other as he faced the fire, unconcerned about who he'd offended tonight. That woman had been whispering about him, just like everyone else tended to do. "The innocent ought not be allowed to wander alone into a dragon's den. And I ought never to have come."

"Of course, you should attend my ball, Sebastian. I swear you'll never come out from the cloud of scandal and marry well the way you are going," Esme huffed, settling back to study him as if he was something she could fix.

"My dear, whoever said I wanted to be married?" he said. "I enjoy my diversions immensely."

"Seducing proper young ladies is not a diversion. Finding a wife should be your goal this season."

Sebastian shook his head. "Your husband may have met his match in you, but that does not mean the rest of us need to. Women are capricious, stubborn, and close-minded. I've enough to deal with at home as it is."

"Gabby is none of those things."

"Gabby?"

"Miss Gabriella Kimble," Esme pointed toward the door. "The girl you just frightened half to death. She's my cousin Bennett's ward."

Gabby. Well, at least he had a name to match the silly pair of lips espousing to admire Viscount Brookes. Gabby. Small in stature, but in her eyes, he'd glimpsed a firebrand willing but not quite ready to come out and play.

He should like to see her turn that temper toward that frivolous fop, Brookes, to see what he might make of her. Brookes would probably run rather than stand up to the challenge of taking on a passionate woman like that. She was ripe to be seduced, too.

But Brookes was undoubtedly leading her on, as he did all the other ladies of society. He would never return her feelings. His greatest love was reserved solely for himself.

But because Brookes was so handsome and attentive, the ladies of society just loved him to smile for them, even Esme. He thrived on admiration. It pained him that so few realized. "Poor Gabby."

"Hardly. She has the wits and intelligence to match even you, I suspect. If not for the loss of her parents, I might never have met her."

Sebastian refused to offer the required sympathy for a poor orphan and scoffed. "She's an idiot, too, if she's set her heart on Viscount Brookes."

Esme's face fell. "I have faith that it is merely a passing infatuation with his good looks."

"Foolish girl," he complained, and then shifted in discomfort. He was already dealing with the results of one foolish infatuation at home and that was enough trouble. "She'll learn the error of her ways in the end. They all do."

"Let's hope it is sooner rather than later, and about you too," Esme murmured.

"I hardly care what she or anyone thinks of me," he insisted.

Esme winced. "How is Cordelia today?"

"The same. My sister keeps to herself and even prepares her own fire rather than let a servant into her rooms to do the task. If I wish to eat in her company, I am forced to dine in her chambers now, too," he complained.

"She's getting worse," Esme said softly.

"It seems so," Sebastian answered, and then tipped his head up to look at the ceiling rather than face the countess' pity. He lowered his face eventually and thumped his fist on the arm of the chair. "At least she stopped barricading her door against everyone. Once the London servants learned to leave her be, she's slowly settled down."

"What will you do?"

"If I listen to the so-called experts I consulted, they offered two solutions for her condition—send for a physician to bleed her extensively or commit her to Bedlam."

"And you won't do either, I know." Esme worried her lip. "She needs to meet more people."

"Hardly possible when she runs and hides from anyone who visits my town house or the estate," he warned. "Even you couldn't get an audience with her still today, and she's known you forever."

"If only she had met someone to marry in her first season this might all have been avoided." Esme made an unhappy face. At the time of her last call, they had only just arrived in

London, and it had gone badly. Cordelia had mumbled and put Sebastian between them and then claimed fatigue so she could flee to her chambers to rest. She stayed there for three days straight, refusing to see all callers.

She'd been miserable about a return to London, but then she would not allow Sebastian to leave her behind either. He'd thought that was a positive sign at the time of their departure from his country estate. Now, though, he knew a change of scenery had done her no favors, or him either.

"Perhaps if you married, a wife might offer her a more stable companionship," Esme suggested, gently. "She'd eventually become accustomed to the woman always being around and might not worry so much about any visitors."

"Making a marriage will solve nothing and could make things ten times worse," Sebastian warned. "Stop trying to inflict a wife on me. I've no time for more than a casual dalliance these days."

"It's not fair to you to put your life on hold," Esme said, wincing.

"I am not complaining about the lack of permanent lovers in my life. Especially not when my last mistress insisted that slipping Cordelia laudanum would keep her calm and out of my way. I ended our relationship in the very next breath, I might add. No, it is better to keep things the way they are now."

"I still say you need someone to help you. Someone to confide in. Not just a physician or the distraction of a lover, but a true companion who you can talk to about these problems, someone who understands what you are faced with each and every day."

"Esme," he growled softly, but then the door to an

adjoining room opened and her husband strode in, grinning from ear to ear.

"Mamble, I've come to save you from my wife's machination. Drink?"

Windermere was merely teasing his wife, but he wasn't wrong. Esme wanted to help but there wasn't much she could do besides suggest he get *more* help. She would prefer he take a wife, while Sebastian had good reasons for not agreeing with her suggestion. "Yes, please," he said with a heavy sigh.

Esme stood with a smile. "Well, I've spoken my mind again and I'll leave you two alone now to recover. Give my love to Cordelia in the morning," she said and then gave her husband a warm smile. "Windermere, do something to make him smile, but try to remember we're hosting a ball, and they are your friends out there as well."

The pair kissed before Esme hurried out the door to oversee her party.

Sebastian scowled as the door closed behind her. "You know, sometimes, I'm not sure I forgive you for marrying that woman and bringing her deeper into our circle."

"Best decision I ever made," Windermere promised with a laugh. "She's usually not wrong when she gives me advice. Of course, I don't always act on it as fast as she cares for."

"Well, she's hell-bent on seeing me leg-shackled this season," Sebastian grumbled to his oldest friend.

"It's not all bad, you know. Being married. There are worse fates for a man than having a wife to wake up with," Windermere promised with his usual smug and satisfied smile that always appeared when he spoke of his beloved Esme.

"Yes, syphilis springs to mind," Sebastian suggested.

"At least you still possess a sense of humor," Windermere said, laughing as he sat himself down finally. "Get married in your own good time, Mamble. You'll suffer no matchmaking efforts from me now or ever in the future."

"Then I guess we will remain friends, despite your marriage to a woman determined to make me a match," Sebastian conceded.

He did like Esme as a friend. She had offered sound advice on many occasions. Windermere was also a good man as well and deserved to be happily married. He'd been a valued confidant for many years. Of course, now, Windermere admitted freely, Esme was his first concern. But adjustments had to be made when good friends finally settled down.

And that future was ahead for him, too, one day, but not now.

Sebastian might tell others he would not marry, but the truth was that until Cordelia either improved or her living situation changed, his solitary path was carved in stone. He would not bring a wife home only to have her demand the removal of his sister, because Cordelia was highly unsocial and prone to bouts of sadness. He would not treat his sister as meanly as his parents had done by locking her up, either. They were the reason why Cordelia was the way she was now.

Cordelia panicked around his guests, was unwilling to leave the town house, and was determined never to let anyone stand close to her. She was unfit for the delights of the London season entirely. Many a family had carted such a problematic daughter off to Bedlam without a qualm. But their father had already tried that and made Cordelia ten times worse.

When Sebastian had inherited the dukedom, his first action was to fetch Cordelia home again and promise she never had to go anywhere she didn't want to go. And she didn't. She had kept to her room for that entire first month, refusing to see anyone—sometimes even him.

Everyone whispered that he kept Cordelia a prisoner. The truth was, she'd made herself her own prisoner. And there was nothing he could do about her *or* the gossip that labeled him cruel.

A few trusted confidants knew the truth. Friends like the Windermeres, who were patient and forgiving of Cordelia's fleeting their company when they called on him at home.

He and Windermere talked and made plans to meet the next day at the club, but Windermere could not stay long in the library. He hurried out to support his wife and mingle with his other guests, leaving Sebastian alone...away from the whispers and accusing stares.

He should never have come. Ten minutes circulating the ballroom had excited the whispering again.

Rumor claimed that he had also banished his younger sister to the countryside. In Rosalind's case, she'd gone off to marry her secret childhood sweetheart—with Sebastian's blessing. Father, of course, had forbid the match to the softly spoken and poor gardener. But Sebastian had known separating them would solve nothing. Rosalind might have married far beneath her status, but she was loved and *in* love, and that was all that ever mattered to Sebastian, especially after learning what Cordelia had been put through.

He should have been with Cordelia when his older sister

had had her disastrous first season. If he'd been the duke, he could have prevented so much misery. But he'd been in school still, oblivious and enjoying himself far too much with his friends. He'd come home to find her gone, and when he found her again, she was completely changed. Almost unrecognizable.

Sebastian burst to his feet, annoyed that his one night away from Cordelia still hadn't emptied his mind of regret and worry about her situation. He set his glass aside, largely untouched, and stood looking down at the fire for a moment. Sitting about in Windermeres library had only made him maudlin. He ought to rejoin the party and at least try to enjoy himself while he could.

He strolled from the library and into the ballroom again, braced to ignore the whispers and stares that followed him everywhere, but his eyes fell immediately on Gabby Kimble...and the whispers suddenly dimmed in their importance.

The little woman was staring forlornly at Lord Brookes, and obviously so.

Sebastian groaned and easily guessed the viscount had not noticed Gabby or asked her to dance.

He looked away and adjusted his cuffs, irritated with her behavior. It reminded him too much of what he'd learned of Cordelia's actions during her first season. Following a fellow around at balls, seeking him out for private conversation. Of course, the fellow had no honorable intentions, but Cordelia hadn't realized that for quite some time.

There were so many better men in society who did want to marry, and Gabby Kimble was doing herself no favors by waiting for a disinterested man to grant her a crumb of his attention.

She ought to be mingling, meeting new people, but of course that required her to notice other men, and be granted introductions to the ones who might help her stand out of the crowd. All she needed was an ally in the room. And not just other women, either. She needed a man to notice her appeal.

Sebastian had noticed her, but *they* hadn't actually been introduced yet.

He thought of turning away, as so many had from Cordelia in her season after rumors had begun about her and gritted his teeth. He might have enjoyed shocking Gabby in the library, but out here, he could not turn her attention elsewhere without drawing attention. Yet any conversation they had, any dance they shared, might help this one woman make a match with someone who deserved her admiration.

And he suddenly wanted to do something truly reckless.

Esme was not far from Gabby Kimble, and Sebastian went to her and immediately leaned down to whisper in her ear, "Introduce me to the kitten."

"Yes, of course," Esme whispered back excitedly and drew him there by his arm, no doubt leaping to a wrong impression of why he wanted the introduction.

It took a moment to drag Gabby's attention away from admiring Lord Brookes, and that irritated him beyond belief.

She seemed surprised to see him standing before her again, but Esme had a knack for smoothing over any awkwardness as the introductions were made. "Miss Kimble, may I introduce my dear friend Sebastian Spence, the Duke of Mamble, to you," she said loudly for all to hear, and beamed a smile for the crowd as well.

Behind Gabby, a pair of gentlemen immediately straightened to attention. Lord Throsby was known to Sebastian already and, beside him, a new face in Town. But judging by the similarity of his features to Gabby's, he was the cousin and guardian Esme had already mentioned.

Miss Kimble dipped a quick, shallow curtsy and smiled. "A pleasure to make your acquaintance, your grace."

He liked that her curtsy was shallow and her response brief and to the point, rather than babbling about the honor like so many women seemed to find necessary with a duke. Sebastian's reputation might be besmirched with false accusations of his misdeeds, but no one ever forgot he was a duke, with a vacancy for a duchess—years overdue to be filled. "And yours."

Esme, of course, had to introduce him to the pair of dumbstruck debutants flanking Gabby, and the unknown man, her cousin and guardian, Mr. Bennett Kimble. But it was clear to see that Gabby was the leader of their little group. They all looked to her for signs of how to react to his introduction.

As the next set was called, Sebastian glanced at the dance card Gabby clutched so tightly to her waist. She seemed anxious and not at all excited about the next set forming. Did she not have a dance partner for this set either?

If she was focusing all attention on the unworthy Lord Brookes, few gentlemen might have had a chance to approach her if she never looked away from him. It wasn't normally in Sebastian's nature to fret about debutants and their lack of dance partners, but he could do her popularity more good by dancing one set with her tonight.

"Miss Kimble, might I tempt you to take the floor with me for the next dance?"

Her friends were instantly delighted on her behalf, but not Gabby. In fact, her eyes narrowed on him with sudden suspicion. "I *should* be honored."

Should be honored? He almost laughed out loud as that bit of sarcasm slipped off her tongue. The tongue that had innocently touched his finger no more than twenty minutes ago. He was right about her. She was no wilting wallflower, and she didn't trust him.

Clever girl.

No one seemed to notice her bright blush as she regarded him for several long moments, sizing him up. He had the ridiculous urge to laugh again. When she eventually handed over her card, he added his name to a completely blank page.

He handed it back with a flourish and held out his hand to her.

Gabby's touch was light in his grip and a strange whisper of anticipation thrummed through his entire being as he led her to the floor. He had perhaps enjoyed too much the speculation and temptation she had stirred in him in the library.

Gabby was an innocent, but her reactions to him had been honest. He'd flustered her well and truly, but not enough to make her flee him...or encourage him, either. He ruthlessly quashed any disappointment over the latter, but it was probably for the best.

Their dance was to be a quadrille, which meant they could talk to each other, but not too often. He led her to their position and then turned to her to bow. "Have you been close to Lady Windermere all of your life?"

"I've only known her a week. We first met at Lady Triscot's ball," she murmured. "It was quite a surprise for my cousin Bennett when he saw her there. He had not seen her for a very long time, I believe."

Sebastian had not attended that ball or heard the Triscots had returned to Town, either. But Esme knew everyone and everything worth knowing. "Are you enjoying tonight's ball still?"

"I am, thank you," she said, her voice warm and her eyes demurely downcast.

He'd rather have her looking at him than faking modesty. "And the season in general? It is your first, isn't it?"

"Yes, the season is everything I expected. Agreeable," she promised, glancing around the room and smiling. "With one recent exception."

That remark did make him laugh out loud.

Sebastian glanced around the room. The foolish Lord Brookes was braying like a donkey and torturing other ladies with his presence across the room. He seemed hardly aware that Miss Kimble even existed.

Not knowing the extent of Gabby's abilities on the dance floor, Sebastian remained watchful as they began the first steps. But it was clear to see Gabby was no bumbling beginner. She moved with utter confidence as she crossed the set to change partners again and again.

Sebastian had to admit he was grudgingly impressed with Gabby's poise by the time their dance neared its conclusion, too. She was in no way in awe of the honor that dancing with a duke might be to others. He was enjoying himself, which was unusual lately, given his problems at home.

"You're a fine dancer," he whispered, hoping to bolster her confidence further.

"So are you," she whispered back, a little more color pinking her cheeks. "It was kind of you to ask me to dance after..."

"I was in the mood," he suggested. He would not have her read too much into his interest toward her tonight.

Her eyes narrowed on him slightly. "I was in a similar state of mind," she promised, and then laughed.

The sound, a delicate invitation to share in her amusement, reminded him of how much he'd enjoyed teasing the young woman in the library. She employed no tactics to lure a man in, but he found himself grinning back.

As they began the promenade to finish the set off, he heard the whispers grow louder as they passed others in the crowd. *Who was she? Where did they meet? Does she know about him?*

Sebastian gritted his teeth and did his best to ignore the whispers and stares as they finally came to a stop and bowed to each other.

Sebastian led Gabby back to where he'd found her, among her friends and guardian, and bowed over her gloved hand. "Miss Kimble, I do thank you for a pleasant dance."

When he rose, he observed a few bachelors of his acquaintance craning their necks and paying more notice to Gabby Kimble. Including Lord Brookes. The viscount had finally lifted his head from his circle of female admirers to see what everyone else was staring at.

Yet Brookes was not looking at Gabby, but at Sebastian...

and for one brief moment, a look of bafflement appeared on the stupid man's face. It lasted for the blink of an eye and then that foolish smile of Brookes' slammed fast back into place.

Gabby cleared her throat, subtly trying to tug her fingers out of his grip without anyone noticing he held her too long. He let her go, and she smiled brightly. But it was a smile that was utterly calculated to fool the world around them.

"Your grace, I would like to express my deepest gratitude for the honor of sharing a dance with you this evening. I do hope we might dance together again soon."

He pursed his lips at her bold suggestion, aware that her popularity, and perhaps her very future in society, hinged on his response. Miss Kimble was aware they had an audience, and he could tell she was hopeful of a positive response from him. Cheeky morsel. Yet he could not commit to anything that might lead to any expectations arising. "Perhaps."

Gabby Kimble curtsied deeply. "Until next we meet."

"Yes, until tomorrow," he replied, surprising himself. Tomorrow, he would make a call on her for the sake of politeness and it might seem to others that he was engaged in a pursuit—but he would make it clear to Miss Gabby Kimble that he certainly was not.

He bowed and strode away, though for some reason he itched to look back over his shoulder to see her face one last time. Miss Kimble was refreshingly direct, and he'd always liked confident women.

Yet, with his dance and his call tomorrow he would set a lure for other gentlemen to discover why Gabby Kimble was the one who had captured the Duke of Mamble's attention tonight.

Well pleased with himself for the deception he would play upon society, Sebastian sauntered away in search of other amusements.

As he passed into the hall, a voice called out. "Well, if it isn't the Duke of Mamble?"

Sebastian spun about and grinned to see Lord Triscot. His old friend hadn't changed in the many years since they'd seen each other. Triscot had been traveling constantly of late, without revealing where he'd taken himself off to, though. Sebastian was wiser than most and did not ask. Triscot had forever been secretive.

They shook hands vigorously. "It's good to see you again."

Triscot merely laughed. "What on earth were you doing dancing with a debutant?"

Sebastian grinned. "A fleeting sacrifice for a worthy cause."

Triscot's eyes lit up. "Did you find her as intriguing as I did?"

Yes, but he would not admit to that out loud. Triscot was not in the market for a wife, anyway. "Just another proper young lady meant to be leg-shackled."

Triscot laughed. "Well, at least my mother has not lost her instincts."

Curiosity got the better of him. "What does your mother say about Miss Kimble?"

Triscot grinned. "Mama claimed I could not do better."

High praise indeed, but Sebastian frowned at the comment. Gabby and Triscot would make a poor match. "*She* could do better than both of us combined."

Triscot readily agreed. Relieved, he took Triscot to the

library to toast their reunion. As he poured some of Windermere's finest whiskey into tumblers, his thoughts returned to Gabby Kimble. She was a mere kitten, but with claws that could be coached out to scratch a man's back if circumstances were right. Too inexperienced to perhaps understand when she was being led astray, too, so she could wind up ruined or married to someone truly unworthy.

Better not to be married at all than badly, in his opinion.

He winced. However, he'd no intention of being cast into the role of matchmaker for anyone, let alone Gabby Kimble —but even as he tried to dismiss her he also knew he would keep an eye on the young woman.

Chapter Three

Gabby looked up as her cousin hurried into their drawing room at last, adjusting his cravat. "About time!"

Bennett met her gaze levelly. "You know, I much preferred you before this season turned you into a fanatic about punctuality."

"Well, it's your own fault. I could kiss you for making my dream of a London season come true," she said sweetly.

"No need for threats or violence," he warned, waving her off and then dropping into his favorite chair across the room. "I always knew you couldn't stay a little girl forever, certainly not under my roof."

Gabby had known Bennett all her life. He had been her guardian since she was eleven and they were like brother and sister after so many years of knowing each other—including squabbling when no one was listening in.

He was the reason she was in London for her first season. Her family had possessed little money, and her dowry was small. But Bennett had made his fortune young and liberally spoiled her. He'd made all her dreams possible last night, too, by accepting his cousin's invitation to a ball, though she shuddered to think what this was costing him. She wanted to marry quickly and well, so he could have his life back. So much depended on her making a good impression in the coming weeks.

Gabby set her hands to her face and let out a shaky breath to calm herself. It was almost time for morning calls, and she expected to have more than one gentleman in their parlor today, not just the rather distracting Duke of Mamble.

Mamble would never choose her to be his bride, and for too many reasons to list, but others might consider her because of his presumed interest.

After all, she had been the only woman chosen by the duke to dance with, and many other gentlemen had paid gratifying attention to her after that. Asking her to dance, others seeking an introduction. There had been plenty of others looking her way after the duke had promised to call on her today, too, and not just men. She'd noticed the envy directed her way by other women. "Do I look all right?"

"You look perfectly fine to me," Bennett promised, barely glancing her way.

Gabby was unusually nervous today. The Duke of Mamble had announced his intention to call on her this morning so loud and clear that if he *didn't* come, she'd be utterly humiliated. "What if he forgets? What if no one else comes?"

"Then they can hardly consider themselves gentlemen. Don't worry. You made quite the impression last night," Bennett promised. "But I'm really all the company you should ever require in the parlor on any morning."

She poked her tongue out at him and then laughed at his exaggerated shock.

"Much better," he announced with an approving nod for her childishness. "Try not to be so serious over all this and do try to have fun."

"Easy for you to say," she grumbled. "If a lady does not

make her match by her second season, you know she will be considered on the shelf. A first season marriage would be best."

"That is not strictly true, and you know it. I'm not worried about you making a match this season. You're being courted by a duke, after all."

"I'm not being courted by the Duke of Mamble," Gabby swore. "He could have no real interest in me."

That man was a study in contradictions, though. She could not quite decide what he was about. Calling her kitten, touching her lips, and then warning her away in the next breath.

Then asking her to dance when no one else had bothered.

He'd saved her evening from being a complete disappointment and made the other gentlemen notice her. She was very grateful, but she suspected now that he was merely amusing himself by pretending to be interested.

She hadn't spotted him again after their dance was over. It was all she could do not to watch for him by the window now, too.

It was foolish to hope, but there was something about him that set him apart from the other gentlemen she'd spoken with in London. It must be the suit he wore so well. He was a cut above all others, and especially her.

Gabby smoothed her gloved hands over her prettiest muslin gown and took a deep breath as she heard the door knocker sound through the house. She knew what to expect from the morning—a brief interlude with a handful of gentlemen who had danced with her last night. She had no faith that Lord Brookes would be among them. He hadn't asked her to dance and had taken the floor with Justine instead, much to her consternation.

Justine said later that he'd asked her to dance when Gabby had been absent from the ballroom. That must have been when she'd slipped into the library, looking for a chance to talk to him in private, and found the Duke of Mamble instead.

A mistake that was perhaps not quite in her best interests when it came to catching Brookes' notice. Many might have considered her compromised. She would be if anyone learned she'd tasted the duke's bare fingertip, too.

She blushed even now, astonished by her own actions toward a gentleman she'd heard nothing good about.

Their butler, Tibbs, announced her third dance partner, Lord Triscot, had arrived. He came bearing lilacs, which Gabby admired and reluctantly set aside. Triscot was whip-thin and smiled a lot as he greeted her cousin. Bennett knew the man from long before Gabby had become his ward.

Triscot turned a beaming smile her way. "How are you today, Miss Kimble?"

"I am very well, my lord. I trust your mother is in good health?"

"Indeed, she is, and sends her warmest regards."

"Do pass along mine as well to her." Gabby leaned a little toward him. "I have it on good authority that you might have purchased a new mount recently."

"That good authority could only have been my dear mama," he replied with a resigned sigh. "I tell you, be glad not to have a mother who can never keep a secret."

Gabby winced. "Was buying a new mount meant to be so great a secret?"

"No, but now she's told you, I've nothing left to say on the subject," he complained, rubbing at his brow.

Gabby smiled quickly. Lady Triscot was a kind woman, but talkative. Gabby had met her several times since coming to London. "She was interrupted before she could launch into a *full* description of the animal."

"That must be a first." Triscot grinned again. "Nineteen hands, black as night but with a settled temperament that makes him easy to ride. A rarity in a stallion."

"He sounds wonderful," she enthused. "I must confess I've ridden nothing but plodding short horses. Sixteen hands at most. I lay the blame squarely at my guardian's feet."

Triscot laughed, but then rubbed his brow. "Then he has done his duty well to protect you from misadventure," he murmured. "I'll have to invite you and your cousin to join me for a ride one day soon."

Gabby glanced over at Bennett for his reaction to that almost invitation. He merely nodded. "Gabby will do well on any mount once she becomes used to being so far from the ground."

"Despite my cousin's claims, I am not afraid of heights," she argued, determined Triscot thought well of her.

"That must have been some other ward of mine, shrieking and stuck up a ladder, clinging to the rails for dear life—" Bennett's words abruptly cut off. "I say, Triscot, are you well?"

"A sudden headache," Triscot promised with a shake of his head. Bennett and Triscot spoke of horses and riding, and a date was set for the pair to go the next week. Triscot took his leave not long after, claiming he was headed back to bed until his sore head passed.

Another gentleman called and took his place, then another, and another.

Bennett began to chuckle after the last one left. "And you feared awkwardness. You handled those gentlemen as if they called on you every day."

"I thought it would be nerve-racking, but men do like to talk about themselves if encouraged. What would you suggest except asking about their most recent purchases?"

"I suppose you could have complimented Triscot on his dancing, except he stomped on your foot, I believe."

"He did, but he apologized immediately." In truth, her best dance partner had been the Duke of Mamble. He had not made a wrong step, and she'd felt herself floating when she was in his arms. Triscot had stumbled about and there was a strong scent of spirits on his breath late last night, which likely explained his sore head today.

A knock sounded, and after a moment, the butler stepped inside, carrying flowers. "These were sent by a Mr. Brown, along with a note for Miss Kimble."

Gabby took the note first and broke the seal to scan the page. "I regret a prior appointment prevents me from calling upon you this morning. Please accept my sincere apology and wish to call on you tomorrow instead."

Gabby exhaled and passed the note to her cousin to read. "I liked him. He made me laugh."

"Well, that is all that is needed in a husband besides a weighty pocketbook," Bennett teased. "Brown will be here tomorrow, never fear. He is renowned for never breaking his word."

"Well, that is very much to his credit," she murmured,

and then took the flowers from Tibbs, who had remained holding them still. "Thank you, sir."

She had liked Mr. Brown, but there had been none of that sudden spark she'd experienced when she'd laid eyes on Lord Brookes, or even the Duke of Mamble.

She had two more callers, both polite and interesting gentlemen, after that. She found herself repeating the same pleasantries and questions to each gentleman, and they went on their way with a professed hope to see her again at a future social engagement.

The door knocker boomed through the house then. Tibbs scampered back to his post to answer it, and Gabby set her flowers aside.

Tibbs returned. "Viscount Brookes."

Gabby could not hide her surprise at the news. Brookes hadn't been expected, but he was the one man she had truly hoped to see in their parlor.

She put on her most pleasing smile. "Do show him in."

Tibbs glanced at Bennett. "He wishes to speak with Mr. Kimble first, and alone."

Bennett frowned and stood, tugging down his waistcoat. "Does he now? Well, you may show the viscount to my study. I'll see him there in a moment."

Gabby waited until Tibbs was gone before she spoke up. "What could he want to say to you in private?"

"I don't know," Bennett said, frowning a little.

"Bennett, what will you say if he asks for my hand in marriage?" she whispered, pulse beginning to race at the prospect. Surely it was too soon to have decided that. But then again, Gabby had fallen for Lord Brookes the moment she'd laid eyes on him.

Bennett stopped beside her chair. "I cannot believe he knows you well enough. Do not get your hopes up. I'll be back in a moment."

Gabby watched Bennett leave and the door fall closed behind him, but she could not remain seated. She crept to the closed door to listen as Lord Brookes was welcomed into the town house and shown to Bennett's study.

Hearing nothing after that, she opened the door a crack wider and set her eye to the gap. The hallway was empty and offered no new information, so she closed it again, turned away and moved toward the front windows.

Lord Brookes' gleaming high-perch phaeton stood outside their town house, attended by only a small boy. Her neighbors across the street were at their windows though, peeking out at the gleaning black and gold carriage, too.

And then a pair of black horses pulling another carriage came into view behind it. Gabby drew back a little, wishing not to be seen by anyone inside. The larger carriage had to stop, and grooms rushed forward to berate the boy holding Lord Brookes' carriage in position on the narrow street-- yelling that it was in the way.

Gabby turned around quickly as the drawing room door creaked open, and Bennett and Lord Brookes strode in one after the other. She quickly rushed back to the center of the room and dipped a curtsey for Lord Brookes. "My lord, welcome."

Brookes beamed a smile her way. "Ah, Miss Kimble. A pleasure to see you here this morning."

"Please, won't you sit down," she said, gesturing to a chair nearby.

"I'm afraid I've not the time to linger today, but it was important to make this call," he said.

Gabby looked at Bennett for guidance, but his expression was inscrutable right now. She would have to wait until Lord Brookes was gone before she could ask about their conversation. Unless...

She turned her best smile on Lord Brookes. "I'm very sorry we did not have an opportunity to speak to each other last night."

"I was too," he promised. "Your friend, Miss Dawes, was a jolly good sort for a dance and swore you had much in common."

Thank you, Justine! "Miss Dawes, and Miss Ellis, too, are the best people I know and the dearest of friends."

"It is good to have good friends," Brookes agreed, glancing at Bennett. "I should hate to attend a party where no one likes each other."

"So would I," she agreed wholeheartedly.

"It is a pleasant day. I was thinking to myself as I arrived that everyone should enjoy the early mornings together in London. A pity balls are not held a great deal earlier."

Gabby laughed softly. "Then it would not be a ball and there would be no need for the candles that make the room seem so magical."

Brookes' smile faltered. "Yes, well, of course. Truly, that would be a shame, too."

"Perhaps you could convince someone you know well to give it a try for you at least once," Bennett suggested dryly.

"Yes. I could ask someone, I suppose," Brookes murmured, seeming a little unsure of himself now. But his smile returned the next moment. "Lady Windermere served a wonderful punch last night. I'm sure you must have tried it."

"Yes, I did have some," she promised. "It was delicious indeed."

Tibbs appeared again, bearing the silver message tray, and walked solemnly toward Gabby. It was clear by the way he held himself that the tray contained something of vital importance.

She swallowed, certain it could only be bad news. "I wonder what this could be."

Tibbs lowered the silver tray so she could read the calling card placed in the exact center. It read *Duke of Mamble*. It was an exquisite calling card. Engraved in gold with little flourishes at the corner.

Gabby gulped and glanced at her cousin, who'd risen to read the card for himself.

"Ah, good," he murmured, giving her a satisfied smile. Bennett addressed Lord Brookes. "About the matter that brought you here, sir. I'm afraid you were quite in error. Thank you for calling."

Bennett seemed determined to have Lord Brookes leave the room immediately, but he did it so well that she was sure Lord Brookes had no idea he'd been gotten rid of.

As soon as he was out of the chamber, Gabby was on her feet and off to the window to peek out again.

Lord Brookes' phaeton was still standing before the house, and a moment later, she watched the viscount leave. But there was no sign of another carriage lined up behind him, not even a riderless horse standing on the street.

Confused by the card and lack of ducal carriage before her house, Gabby discovered she was quite disappointed.

She had looked forward to seeing how the duke would behave today. Last night, it seemed she'd encountered two different men: a rake and a respectful gentleman.

Gabby turned around—and yelped to find the duke standing directly behind her, unannounced by their butler.

She hastily dipped a respectful curtsy. "Your grace."

Mamble was every inch a duke today, and when he smiled, she almost lost her breath, overwhelmed momentarily by that sense of presence about him. His eyes skimmed lazily up and down her body again, too, causing a burst of heat to sweep over her skin.

She struggled not to fidget but found she could bear his bold scrutiny more easily today. "Welcome."

He moved past her and peered outside at the street. "You can thank me later for driving that blithering idiot off, but then I feel sympathy for the poor women he inflicts himself on next."

Gabby shook her head. "It was an honor to be visited by Lord Brookes."

Mamble pursed his lips. "I suppose you want me to apologize for interrupting your little tête-à-tête with a man you admire so well? I had no idea he'd actually stir himself to call on you."

"Why wouldn't he?"

The duke leaned close. "Because he has led too many ladies on for me to imagine he'd choose you, and as charming as you are. I heard he still did not dance with you last night."

"Perhaps he called because I'm irresistible," she shot back, and then winced at how conceited that sounded.

"You *are* interesting, I'll give you that," the duke

whispered. "But not to him yet. He's not the man for you, Gabby."

"I think he could be," she insisted, fighting a blush. She refused to believe that her hopes for Brookes and herself were in vain while ignoring the duke's bold use of her first name. Remembering her manners, Gabby offered him a seat that would put them both in full view of the door. "My cousin should be back at any moment."

"Good. I assure you, I do not want to compromise you." He sat down and leaned back in the chair, crossing one leg over at the knee. "What shall we talk about today? Empty pleasantries again? Did you enjoy the ball last night?"

"I did indeed, and I'm grateful to Lady Windermere for the invitation."

He frowned suddenly. "What were your friends' names again? Their connections?"

"Miss Justine Dawes and Miss Daisy Ellis."

"It is Miss Daisy Ellis who has Throsby as her guardian?"

"Yes. Do you know Lord Throsby?"

"Of course, and the other? Tell me about her connections."

"Miss Justine Dawes. Perhaps you know her sister, Lady Whitlow."

He seemed to stiffen in his chair. "Would that be Lady *Clarissa* Whitlow, viscountess?"

Gabby nodded quickly. "Yes."

The duke pursed his lips. "I see."

"Are you acquainted with the family? I would be happy to introduce you to my friend's sister if you were not."

"I don't care to be introduced to anyone connected to the Whitlows," he said somewhat sternly.

"Oh," Gabby replied, thoroughly confused by his response. "What could be wrong with knowing Justine's family better?"

Bennett strolled in then and the duke didn't answer, but he seemed unconcerned to find Gabby sitting alone with the duke in their front parlor. "Appreciate you keeping your word to call on my ward, your grace," Bennett said, sitting down to join them.

"I said I would come."

Bennett's lips twitched. "And so very loudly, too."

The duke smiled slightly and then glanced her way. "I believe you danced for the rest of the night after our set."

"Yes, I did," she said, and then decided to be blunt about her suspicions. "Did you expect that would happen? That others would follow your example."

"Perhaps I did."

"Thank you." She smiled quickly. "I cannot ever repay you for such a kindness."

"'Twas not a kindness but a remedy for folly," he said briskly.

"Folly?" she said slowly, narrowing her eyes at him. Was he talking about her unchaperoned visit to the library where they'd first met, or her declaration about admiring Lord Brookes?

"What folly was that?" Bennet asked, frowning as he glanced between.

Gabby prayed the duke would not mention meeting her last night. Bennett, who knew of her interest in Brookes but not that she went in search of him for a private conversation, would not be pleased.

Mamble shrugged. "Of my fellow man for being so blind as to ignore your ward."

She let out a shaky breath. Lord Mamble wasn't about to share her secrets with her guardian today.

She smiled at him again, grateful. "Will you be in Town long, your grace?"

"Yes, for some time. Most of the season, I imagine." He turned to Bennett. "I learned from Lord Triscot that you have a long connection to his family."

"Indeed. We knew each other as boys," Bennett admitted. "He was actually the first patient I ever had, and he's never let me forget the pain of the stitches I put into his arm that day."

The duke's eyes narrowed on Bennett. "You're a surgeon?"

"Among other things. It was always my greatest wish to help those in need." Bennett's eyes flickered in her direction. "Of late, I tend the needs of a small country parish. Perhaps you are acquainted with Somerset and Lord Scarsdale's country estate there? We've been friends since childhood."

"We are acquainted but I have never visited him there," Mamble admitted and then suddenly laughed. "You've been away from society a long time, sir."

"Much has changed," Bennett murmured.

Bennett had said very little to Gabby about his life before she'd become his ward but, clearly, he'd enjoyed a wider acquaintance than she'd ever known. She glanced down at her hands as Bennett's enthusiasm for the subject of the past loosened his tongue and guilt set in. Bennett had given up his life to take care of her in the country.

"And what of you, Miss Kimble?" The duke asked, startling her. "Have you performed in as many amateur theatricals, too?"

She glanced at Bennett, startled by the question and by what she must have missed of the conversation.

"No," she told the duke. "No one has ever asked me before."

"Well, perhaps someone will one day," Mamble murmured. "Although treading the boards is considered scandalous for unmarried ladies."

"I am never afraid to consider something new," she told the duke.

"I would never let you make a fool of yourself the way I did," Bennett assured her.

Mamble nodded, seemingly satisfied with that promise. "Kimble, perhaps you would care to join me for luncheon and cards tomorrow. Just a gathering of some friends away from the prying eyes of the *ton*."

"That is very generous of you, but I would not like to impose."

"It will be no imposition, I assure you," Mamble promised. "Windermere will be there and I'm sure he'll be glad for your inclusion."

"Thank you, but I would rather hear it from his lips first," Bennett said more cautiously now, though clearly still keen to go.

Gabby immediately fretted that such an outing for cards might give Bennett a taste of something his pocketbook could not afford right now. The duke's circle had unlimited funds for gambling, but Bennett did not. Especially not when he had the expense of her first season to pay for. She'd heard of the outrageous wagers placed in the gentlemen's club betting books. She shuddered to think what was fritted away in private.

They talked a little more about meeting each other, Bennett receiving the details of the luncheon, and then the duke asked, almost as an afterthought, if she would be attending the Pendleberry ball.

Behind the duke's back, Bennett was urging her to confirm their invitation, although Gabby knew nothing of the ball yet. "I'm looking forward to it. Will your sister be there?"

The duke's smile vanished in an instant. "Perhaps."

"I hear she is a remarkable woman," Gabby added, watching the duke closely. "I should love to make her acquaintance."

The duke's expression turned even more guarded. It was as if a wall had crashed down between them. He stood. "Well, then. Mr. Kimble, Miss Kimble. Until we meet again."

Gabby hastily dipped a curtsy as Bennett escorted Mamble out of the room, and he was out of the house within minutes.

She rushed to the window to see him go off on foot, not even bothering to return his hat to his head.

Bennett groaned. "Why did you have to mention his sister?"

"His *prisoner*."

"You should not believe everything you hear, Gabby,"

Bennett warned. "There could be more going on there than we know."

"What more is there to know? He never lets his sister mingle with society. We have to help the poor lady escape."

"Cordelia," Bennett muttered, raking a hand through his hair. "Her name is Lady Cordelia, and I can guarantee she needs no help from us."

She blinked in surprised at the warm way he uttered the lady's name. "Do you know her, Bennett?"

"I was in London during her season."

"You never told me that before," Gabby said as she moved around to face her cousin. "That you enjoyed a season."

"I was not here for all of it," Bennett said. "I had to leave when my father died."

Gabby winced. "And then you were burdened with me not long after that."

"It was a horrible few years for both of us," he said, patting her shoulder. He glanced around. "Do you think that's the last of your callers today?"

"Perhaps so."

"Well, if it is, perhaps I can persuade you to accompany me out for an ice."

"I'd like that," she said, and then frowned. "Bennett, what did Lord Brookes want to speak to you about?"

He shrugged. "Some nonsense about Mamble leading you on."

Which was exactly what Mamble had said about Brookes. "But he did come."

"He did indeed," Bennett smiled. "My dear, despite your modesty, I suspect you have an admirer there."

"A duke couldn't possibly be interested in me," she promised her cousin. Not for anything but wickedness, perhaps. "I've not a dowry of the size he must require in a bride, nor the connection to any great family."

"Well, stranger things have happened. You are related to Lady Windermere and her husband is a good friend of his."

"It is a tenuous connection we have with Lady Windermere at best," she cautioned her cousin.

"All I'm saying is that not every man does what society expects of us," Bennett promised. "Mamble never has."

While Gabby appreciated her cousin's faith in her abilities to bring a duke up to scratch, she was a realist at heart. Her lack of fortune excluded her from the lofty ambition of becoming a duchess. She had to be reasonable in her expectations for her season. She required a husband with a bit of wealth and a kind, happy temperament.

Mamble had only sought an introduction, danced with her, because of their rather scandalous exchange in the library.

However, the duke had done her one great favor by dancing with her last night and calling on her today. But it was not something she could imagine him ever repeating. Lord Brookes had the right of it. The Duke of Mamble would only disappoint her in the end if she thought too much of his interest.

Chapter Four

"ARE YOU GOING OUT AGAIN?"

Sebastian froze halfway down the stairs, late for the ball he'd promised to attend, and looked up. His sister Cordelia was watching him from a higher landing. He hadn't seen her out of her chambers all day and she chose *now* to show her face? At the very last moment?

"The Pendleberry Ball is tonight," he told her. "I had promised to go last week. You had an invitation, too. I asked if you would join me, but you declined."

"I forgot that was tonight," Cordelia whispered, rubbing her brow. "I'll see you tomorrow then."

"Yes, for breakfast as usual," he agreed.

Sebastian started each day making sure Cordelia got out of bed and dressed, even if she wouldn't see anyone. For a while, months, she hadn't done either one. She'd slept heavily, but that couldn't and shouldn't have gone on forever. "Or we could go riding together in the morning like we used to do, if you'd prefer," he suggested, though he didn't hold out much hope she'd agree.

Cordelia shook her head and fled back toward her chambers. She did not agree to any of his suggestions to go out with him, but still he persisted in reminding her of the fun they used to share. There was a whole world outside she ought to be a part of, but she never could be unless she wanted to.

Sebastian sighed heavily and then continued down the stairs to where the butler waited with his hat and gloves at the ready for his evening out. He was running late because Cordelia had picked at her dinner earlier and he'd lingered, waiting her out until she'd eaten sufficiently enough to sustain her.

The butler pretended nothing was wrong, but Sebastian was certain he had taken note of the exchange with Cordelia on the stairs. "Keep an eye on her movements about the house tonight."

"As ever, your grace," he promised. Sometimes Cordelia lingered on the stairs. The London servants were as concerned about Cordelia's state of mind as Sebastian was. They had been here for her first and disastrous season and must see the difference in her very plainly.

They probably knew what father had done with her after, as well. Everyone who knew Cordelia worried about her fragile state of health. Yet nothing they'd done so far seemed to have any impact or bolstered her confidence.

He pulled on his gloves, frustration making his shoulders hitch up. "Send up a plate of strawberries around eleven and tell her they were from me," he asked.

"It will be done," the butler promised. "If I might suggest an addition. Lady Cordelia used to enjoy hot chocolate in the evenings. Shall I send that up too."

Cordelia ate like a sparrow, and it was beginning to show. Her face was becoming drawn and her hands were always cold when he touched them. Yet the more he pushed her to eat, the more stubbornly she refused. "No. You may ask if she'd care for it but leave the decision to her. She must interact with the servants more," he replied.

"As you wish," the butler murmured, stepping aside to open the front door for Sebastian.

Sebastian's carriage was waiting at the bottom of the steps, and he hurried to climb inside. He was not truly in the mood for the merriment of a ball, but he'd promised to put in an appearance. The hostess was a family friend, eager to have her ball be a success or at least made notorious with his attendance. After his brief appearance at the ball, Sebastian would likely head to his club to end the evening with masculine conversation before heading home to Cordelia.

Lady Pendleberry's excitement to have him finally appear in her front hall was obvious when he arrived, and she rushed him into the ballroom immediately so everyone would see him. Guests turned around to acknowledge his arrival, but then the whispers and stares began.

From all but two, that was.

The *kitten* was in attendance, watching him from across the room again as she stood beside her cousin and guardian, Bennett Kimble. He'd forgotten the Kimbles could be in attendance, but of course, with their connection to Lady Windermere, doors that had once been previously shut to the pair were now widening.

Sebastian avoided Miss Kimble by walking in the opposite direction. He was determined not to pay her too much notice, but in a ball of this small size, it was impossible that they could ignore each other for the entire night.

Their first words were during a set he had not been able to avoid participating in.

Gabby was partnered with another gentleman opposite,

and Sebastian met her in the center of the dance floor. "Miss Kimble."

"Your grace," she murmured back as she took hold of his hand to spin about.

Sebastian experienced a jolt of awareness at the contact that he did not usually feel around other women. When she returned to her proper partner, he noticed her cheeks were flushed a delicate shade of pink, too. When she noticed him observing her still, the color grew far more pronounced.

Was that from exertion, or was she thinking of their interlude in the library a week ago?

He acutely remembered the brush of her tongue against his fingertip. The memory had caused a rather wicked fantasy as he'd waited for sleep to claim him each night since.

The set ended, but there was some commotion near Gabby, and he saw her limp from the dance floor, aided by her stammering dance partner. She returned to her cousin, and then disappeared alone for a while.

Sebastian spoke pleasantries to his last dance partner, but his curiosity and concern grew the longer Gabby was gone from the room. It made him wonder if Lord Brookes had been invited, and if the woman was attempting to speak with him alone again somewhere in the house again. The thought of Gabby and Brookes engaged in any sort of flirtation left a decidedly unpleasant taste in his mouth.

But after several minutes, Gabby limped back to her guardian's side and began to whisper to him. Whatever was said in response made her shake her head, and then she faced the dance floor with a smile that was clearly strained.

She peeked at him from under her lashes a few too many

times for him to ignore though. Was she attempting to flirt with him or, despite the limp, encourage him to ask her to dance again tonight?

He slowly made his way toward Gabby and her guardian, determined to make it clear that he would not be cooperating with that farce. But he could talk to her for a little while.

He thrust out his hand to Kimble, making it clear whose conversation he sought. "Kimble, good to see you again," he said as Gabby dipped a curtsey, slightly more awkward than the last he'd seen her perform. He inclined his head to her but looked back at Kimble quickly.

"Your grace, good evening," Kimble replied. "It's a fine night for a party."

"It is indeed," he agreed. "How did you fare after our luncheon last week?"

"I enjoyed it immensely but not my pounding head the next morning," Kimble remarked. But a small frown crept over his face.

"Is something the matter?"

"No. Most likely its nothing of importance. But I wonder if I might claim an hour of your time tomorrow?" Kimble murmured quietly. "I would not presume to call on you at home, but it could be of great interest to you to hear what I have to say."

Sebastian studied the man and then glanced at Gabby, too, who seemed surprised by her cousin's request for a private appointment. Kimble, by all accounts, was a serious man, and Sebastian paid attention when serious men had concerns. "You may call in the morning. I'm free from nine."

"Thank you," Kimble answered, and with obvious relief,

too. They made small talk until the next set was called. Kimble was to dance with Lady Archer, a widow new to Town, and Sebastian was abandoned and left to continue to stand beside Gabby and watch others pair up.

"You've a partner for this set, yes?" he whispered as their hostess drifted closer, eyeing him and Gabby standing side by side. Any moment, Lady Pendleberry would probably conscript him to dance with Gabby, whether he wanted to or not.

While Gabby was a fine dancer, he was still worried about misunderstandings. He acknowledged he found her attractive, but nothing further could be possible between them.

"I'm afraid I stubbed my toe badly in the last set and cannot dance again tonight, though I long too," she admitted in a whisper.

"I'm sorry to hear that," he answered before the hostess joined them. "Ah, Lady Pendleberry. I meant to say earlier how wonderful you look tonight," he said with a teasing grin. Lady Pendleberry was a handsome woman over fifty, with snow-white hair and a curvaceous figure. She was a kind soul and usually blushed at any compliment he made about her appeal. "If only I were ten years older, I might give your husband a run for his money."

"I'll tell him you said that later." But Lady Pendleberry beamed and then glanced at Gabby suddenly. "Oh, my dear, he means nothing by that. The duke and I are very old friends, and he enjoys teasing me and my husband."

"But, my dear, I do hold you in the highest esteem," Sebastian promised, hand on his heart. "It is my joy to make you blush."

"Now that is something you should do for a much younger lady, who must long for such a passionate declaration as he twirls her about my ballroom," she said, giving Gabby a sideward glance.

Gabby quickly informed the hostess that she was not fit for further dancing tonight.

"Well," Lady Pendleberry huffed, clearly disappointed to hear the news that Gabby could not enjoy the evening more.

"I promise I am content to watch everyone else dance and to talk," Gabby assured the hostess.

Lady Pendleberry beamed. "I'll leave you two to continue your conversation, then. If you need anything, just ask a servant to help you."

"I will," Gabby promised.

Lady Pendleberry moved away, and Sebastian faced the dancers again, standing shoulder to shoulder with Gabby. He couldn't help but notice she was without those little friends of hers. Miss Ellis and Miss Dawes must not have been invited. He was happy about the latter's absence. "Aside from the bruised toe, have you enjoyed your night so far?"

"Very well, thank you. Lady Pendleberry is lovely and very kind," Gabby told him, and then frowned. "She speaks highly of you."

"Yes, she's been very helpful over the years," Sebastian confessed. Lady Pendleberry had given him sound advice from the moment he'd taken Cordelia from the madhouse. Her own family had committed an uncle to Bedlam, and she'd urged him to free Cordelia as soon as possible and to treat her very gently.

"She reminds me of our old neighbor in the country. Forever dropping by to check that I have everything I need," Gabby said, beginning to sway as a new tune started, played by an unseen quartet.

The skirts of her gown brushed his leg, and he smiled to himself. Gabby Kimble probably had no idea the gesture was in any way provocative to gentlemen. "You were orphaned, I hear?"

"Yes, poor Bennett had his hands full when I arrived on his doorstep at just eleven years of age," she said, apparently not the least bit hesitant to confide in him. "He'd just lost his own father and been alone for a mere six weeks at that time. We were both nursing a broken heart. He's been a wonderful guardian."

"And your late father and mother? What were they like?"

"I am ashamed to say I have trouble remembering them clearly now," she whispered. "My mother died when I was very young. I kept my father's pipe and light it occasionally, to remind myself of his scent."

"It is good that you had family to go to and friends that care about your welfare," he murmured. "Kimble seems a decent fellow."

"He is indeed. He's become a friend and confidant. You have your sisters, I believe, though I've never seen either one in Town yet," she said, her brow arched, clearly fishing for information again.

He sighed. What would be the harm in being equally forthcoming? "My younger sister is married, and partakes of London society no more," Sebastian advised. "I'm expecting to hear I am an uncle, any day now."

"How wonderful. And your other sister? Cordelia, isn't it?"

"Correct," he said and felt his spine straighten.

"What is she like?"

His sister was difficult to explain. Once he might have said she was funny and accomplished, but those days were long ago. What could he say about his sister now, to counteract the gossip Gabby had obviously heard about how he treated her? *Oh, my sister might be mad.* No, that would never do.

But given her connection to Lady Windermere, there was every chance he'd see Gabby again and again and be subjected to her constant questions. And it bothered him that she might believe the gossip as well. He did not want this particular young lady to think the worst of him.

Gabby seemed the type to be kind, and perhaps Cordelia might like her enough to actually talk with her one day, were they ever to meet. Given her connection to Lady Windermere, it couldn't hurt to drop a hint of what the real situation was, and, if fate might ever lead to an introduction, it would disprove the gossip with proof.

And if it did not go well, then Gabby would have all the answers she could ever need about his supposed cruelty toward his sister.

But not even Esme could get an interview with Cordelia lately. Not unless she dropped by unannounced. That was the only way Cordelia spoke to anyone outside of him and the servants.

He debated a moment, and then moved a little closer to Gabby to whisper, "Your cousin asked to speak with me tomorrow about a matter of some sort. Come with him in the morning and meet Cordelia yourself, if you can. I'll expect you both at ten o'clock for breakfast."

"I should like that very much," Gabby said instantly, though her brow creased with confusion the next moment.

He'd no more time for conversation with the debutant tonight though. Other guests were already looking his way, and a few brows were being raised at their prolonged discussion. He must mingle before tongues wagged in earnest—even among friends.

He excused himself as the current set ended, found an unpartnered woman keen to dance for the next, and devoted his attention to conversing with her instead.

As they took to the floor, he felt a pang of guilt to see Gabby standing so forlornly beside her guardian. And he realized he'd much rather have danced with her again tonight instead of the woman he was with. But with an injury, of course, Gabby couldn't dance with anyone.

He went through the motions of the dance blindly, and when he looked up again, Gabby was surrounded by a pair of bachelors.

It seemed his attention to Gabby still convinced others of her worth for conversation, at least. He suspected it would continue to happen the more he met with her. Men flocked to what other men found desirable, after all. A pity they could not choose women based on merit alone. But they looked for beauty first and intelligence last. Gabby Kimble seemed to possess both in abundance.

When he finished his set and parted ways with his dance partner, he positioned himself on the opposite side of the room from Gabby. Watching over her since her guardian seemed quite popular with the unmarried ladies tonight.

Despite not dancing, she appeared to be having a marvelous time, and it was clear she had no trouble conversing with other gentlemen.

Sebastian had not enquired about the extent of Gabby's dowry, but, with her connection to the Windermeres, surely, she could do much better than Viscount Brookes.

The pair of bachelors exchanged a glance over her head that suggested they were interested in the debutant—and not in a good way.

He was moving before he realized it. Moving toward Gabby with thoughts of protecting her from the lascivious pair. He stopped himself short of joining them, but the pair noticed his scowl and made excuses to leave her rather suddenly.

Sebastian had paused beside the refreshment table, so he made a request of the servant and discovered Lady Pendleberry was serving only Negus punch. Not a particular favorite of his, but he drank it anyway. When he finished, he had to decide where he should go next. He felt restless and strangely drawn to return to Gabby's side.

He was saved by the hostess. Lady Pendleberry stopped in front of him, scowling. "You're not dancing. Let me find you a partner."

"I'm no longer in the mood to dance," he told her. In truth, he'd not intended to stay this long at all. He'd planned to already be at his club and halfway through a bottle of claret by now, talking about investment or politics to anyone who cared to join him.

He'd lingered because of Gabby.

"Perhaps supper will put you in a dancing mood again,"

she suggested. "Or do you only desire a certain young lady's conversation tonight?"

"I enjoy conversation with ladies of all ages," he promised. "Tell me of your children. I believe your youngest will be making her come out next year."

"That is not the conversation you want to have tonight," Lady Pendleberry whispered, and then winked. "I've known you too long to believe you're still here because of my ball."

He could have denied it, but Lady Pendleberry did know him very well. He was interested in Gabby, but it was not the time or the place for that. He risked making a spectacle of himself and disappointing her.

He bowed to his hostess. "Thank you for a wonderful evening, Lady Pendleberry, but you must excuse me."

"Oh, Mamble. Don't run away yet."

"I promised Cordelia I would not be out too late tonight," he said, fibbing greatly. If he arrived home early, Cordelia probably wouldn't see him, anyway. But he would prefer to return home rather than the alternative of walking across the room and speaking to Gabby again. "Good evening."

"Good evening, your grace. Give my love to Cordelia when you see her in the morning."

"I will," he said before strolling away. He glanced back once before he reached the threshold of the room. Gabby had come to the notice of yet another bachelor. She did not need him.

But then their eyes met across the dance floor, and he saw her disappointment that he was leaving clear as day.

He might have stayed, but he didn't trust his interest in

Gabby Kimble. He did not like that he couldn't trust himself around her.

Chapter Five

"Gabby, would you make haste? We are going to be late!" Bennett called to her from the lower floor.

Her cousin Bennett could be the slowest man in the entire world, but today, Gabby was the one dragging her feet. She was on her way to visit Lord Mamble's home, but it was his sister who she was most worried about meeting.

The prisoner. Although why Mamble would invite her to meet Lady Cordelia still seemed odd to her. But she was going—and she had all the money she possessed tucked into her reticule, and the address of a friend who could harbor Lady Cordelia, should the duke's sister wish to escape his clutches.

She hurried downstairs and into her cousin's carriage, breathless. She took a deep breath once they were underway. Her stomach was full of flutters. How would Mamble behave? Why would he want her to meet his sister?

She was eager to see the duke again, though, bad reputation or not. She had enjoyed their conversation last night. No other gentleman seemed to want to know her opinions the way he did. But it was so odd that the duke had invited them so early that she'd not slept a wink last night.

When they arrived before the grand entranceway, Bennett bounded out of the carriage. Gabby descended more slowly, looking up at the building's facade as her feet touched the ground. Mamble House didn't look like a prison. It was an impressive abode though, just like all the rest in the Grosvenor Square seemed to be.

A smiling butler invited them in and took Bennett's hat and gloves and Gabby's pelisse. He led them toward the back of the building, through a series of twists and turns that thoroughly confused Gabby before they stopped outside a wide set of closed doors.

They entered into a sunny, bright chamber. There was a canary singing in one corner, and a meal on the table. On the far side of the round table stood the Duke of Mamble, and by his side was a woman of incomparable beauty. Gabby had definitely never seen the duke's sister before, or she would have certainly remembered that face. The woman wore a soft green round gown, her blonde hair pulled back from her face and secured at the nape of her neck.

Not a shackle in sight though.

Quickly realizing she was staring at the woman, she glanced at the duke. Mamble was dressed informally this morning. Clad in a navy-blue waistcoat and breeches with a white linen shirt whose sleeves were rolled up to his elbows, he seemed entirely at ease.

Gabby dipped a deep curtsy, but as she rose, she realized something was amiss. Bennett had not bowed.

Mamble remained on his feet, now tense, and there was an odd expression on his face as he looked across at them. Gabby glanced to the side. Bennett was there—staring— clearly struck dumb by their surroundings or the exalted company. She subtly elbowed him, and he stumbled through a smooth recovery that impressed her.

Mamble's shoulders eased down, and he invited them to sit as he introduced his sister, Lady Cordelia.

"It's a pleasure to finally meet you," Gabby said to the woman.

"And you," she replied, then glanced deferentially at her brother.

"Mr. Bennett Kimble and Miss Gabriella Kimble are distant relations of Esme's, Cordelia," he murmured. "Cousins in fact."

"Several times removed," Kimble added quickly. "We were never particularly close, and it was only by chance that we were reunited when we came to London."

"Gabby came out this year," Mamble supplied, when Cordelia only nodded. "You can imagine the plans Esme's making to support her relation's first season, and to make it a great success. It is a pity you could not have met her at the Pendleberry's ball last night."

"I was sorry you were not there, too," Gabby enthused. "It was a wonderful evening, full of dancing and lively conversation."

"I was indisposed," Cordelia murmured, eyes lowering demurely. "I wish you all the luck in the world for your season."

The duke nodded to his sister and then gestured to the table. "We eat informally in the morning, so you will have to make do with me serving you both," he said, moving to the sideboard. "Cordelia, might I offer you another pastry?"

"No, thank you," Cordelia answered swiftly.

He glanced over his shoulder. "Are you sure? Cook has outdone himself today."

"Yes, Sebastian. I am quite sure that I want nothing more today."

"All the more for us then," he said with a heavy sigh. "Would you mind serving my guests tea, or coffee if Mr. Kimble prefers that?"

Gabby saw Lady Cordelia flinch, but she stood and moved around the table, pouring Gabby a cup of strong black tea. Gabby couldn't help but notice that her hands shook, and a drop of tea spilled on the pearly white tablecloth. The woman's breath hitched. Pained and more panicked than it ought to be for such a spill.

Bennett refused tea or coffee, and Cordelia resumed her chair and turned her attention to her plate as if it was the most fascinating thing in the world. But her cheeks were pink from embarrassment over the spilled drop—as if she'd made a terrible faux pas.

When Gabby reached for her teacup to take a sip from, she moved her saucer slightly so the duke would not see the spill when he returned to the table and become cross about it.

The duke brought platter after platter to Gabby and Bennett so they could select what they wanted and tried to get his sister to take an extra helping of eggs, which she refused. Gabby felt a little awkward about the duke waiting on them like a servant, but he merely smiled and brought yet another dish for her to choose from.

She was relieved when he finally sat down to resume his own meal. "My sister and I eat together often. I always tell Cordelia a good meal and conversation sets the right tone for the day," he said.

"You *do* always say that." A tiny smile appeared on

Cordelia's face as she glanced at her brother, but Gabby noticed she was pushing food around on her plate and not eating.

Cordelia was uneasy. Truly, how much of a tyrant could the duke be at home?

"My cousin and I eat together often, as well," Gabby said to Cordelia, hoping to draw her out. "It does set the tone for the day to share a meal with someone you care for. I have such fun planning extravagant birthday dinners for Bennett each year, too."

"She always serves too much food," Bennett confessed, patting his flat stomach. "But it is just once a year, and I appreciate being spoiled as much as the next man."

Cordelia glanced sideways at her brother and frowned. "Sebastian used to enjoy them as well."

Used to? Did he not let her do anything?

"I'm sure you must have hosted some wondrous dinners over the years for him and his closest friends," she said. "I'd love to hear about them sometime. Perhaps I could make Bennett's next birthday even better than the last."

Cordelia mumbled something, but Gabby didn't catch it all, and she dared to ask the woman to repeat herself.

The duke raised a brow and then glanced sideways at his sister, clearly giving her permission to answer the question honestly. Cordelia regarded him for a long time and then mumbled, "He wants me to act as his hostess, but I don't want to."

Gabby's smile slipped. "You don't?"

Cordelia stood abruptly, setting her napkin aside. "Please, you must excuse me."

"Cordelia, please remain," the duke said, almost begging her not to go.

But his sister shook her head. "I will see you tomorrow."

"I'll see you for dinner tonight," the duke countered. Mamble rose and reached for the woman's hand. "Come and find me if you want to talk later. I will be staying in all day, and night as well."

Lady Cordelia's smile was quick and then she excused herself from the room, rushing away so fast she could not have heard Gabby's or Bennett's hasty farewells.

The duke pursed his lips, clearly disappointed she'd gone, and then lowered himself to his chair again with a heavy sigh. "It was worth a try."

Gabby narrowed her eyes at him. "A try?"

The duke's eyes flashed dangerously, and she could tell he was angry with her for speaking out. He rested his arm on the table between them and growled, "She's afraid of *everyone* but me." And then he made a visible effort to control his temper. He moved back and shrugged. "My sister dislikes company. Her black moods can last for weeks. I had wondered, hoped, that an introduction to strangers might spark her curiosity."

Gabby gaped. "Melancholy?"

"I'm sure it's nothing like that." Bennett whispered, leaning toward her.

"Then she is afraid of *him*," Gabby insisted. "Afraid of putting a foot wrong in his presence like the rumors suggest."

"Gabby!" Bennett chided quickly. "She did not mean that, your grace."

The duke met her gaze, and when he spoke, a smile appeared. "Do you really believe Cordelia was kept as my prisoner, like every other fool does? They whisper of my cruelty. Tell everyone I keep her locked up day and night." He shook his head." Of course, you believed *them*. Why else would you so eagerly come? To gawk and stare."

"No one sees her," she whispered.

"*She* won't see people. Not here, not anywhere, unless she is surprised by their arrival like today. Ask Esme how often Cordelia is at home to her. They were close once." Mamble looked past her to address Bennett. "Sir, I believe I promised you a private word. Come along to my study now. Miss Kimble can remain here. I assure you the servants will take good care of her while you are gone. They won't even lock her in."

"Your grace—" she began quickly.

But the duke cut her off with an impatient wave of his hand and a growl of *enough* and headed out the door.

"That was not well done, Gabby. Not well done at all," Bennett chided, and he patted her shoulder awkwardly as he passed her chair, dutifully following the duke from the room for his private meeting.

Gabby kept her back straight until she could no longer hear him and then slumped, filled with shame. She ought to have given him the benefit of the doubt. If she had known more, though, she might not have been so quick to judge, too. Gabby was no stranger to melancholy. Her papa had suffered. Suffered in silence, with only Gabby becoming aware of his struggles much too late to have done him any good.

If Cordelia was afflicted like her own father, then she understood why no one saw the woman. The duke had her sympathy, for what it was worth.

She pushed back from her chair and stood, angry with herself for listening to gossip. For believing Justine and her older sister about the situation here without question. She had wronged the duke and Lady Cordelia, too.

Clearly, the duke liked his sister. They took breakfast together every day and dined together too. He urged her to eat, although the lady had no great appetite. The duke had gently tried to engage her in conversation and begged her to stay.

Gabby paced the room in agitation. Guilt eating her up and wondering what she could do about that. Her friend Justine and others were spreading gossip that was so very wrong.

At Cordelia's chair, she happened to glance down and noticed the napkin that would have been on the woman's lap; it was wrinkled from being twisted by nervous hands. Papa had done that toward the end, too.

Had Gabby and Bennett's arrival been the cause of her anxiety, or was that an everyday habit? Papa had done it every day, and when he was alone, too. He had also refused to let his chambers be cleaned properly, adding more and more possessions with each passing year.

It broke Gabby's heart that a woman as beautiful and gentle as Lady Cordelia appeared to be, could be, afraid of company.

She closed her eyes.

Afraid of her.

Papa had been like that sometimes but, being a man, he could be rude and curt with friends and family and not be thought odd for a long time. Somehow, she had to make things right. She had angered the duke today, and he would be in the right to wash his hands of their acquaintance entirely. She'd proven herself to be no better than a fool. If only she had not assumed the worst of the situation. Yet so many people in society whispered about Mamble—and so unfairly. She must apologize to him and try to make things better between them immediately. She would freely admit that to him today.

Gabby headed for the door and stepped out into the hall. To her right was the twisting path she'd taken to get here.

To the left, the unknown.

But then the duke emerged from a chamber down the hall, striding out to cross to another room with a book in his hand. He saw her standing there and paused, a frown on his face. Gabby squared her shoulders and lifted her chin. "Your grace."

He came toward her slowly, scowling. "Is something wrong, Miss Kimble?"

"Not with me. Not now," she promised, wetting her lips. "I merely wanted to say how very sorry I am that I believed the gossip. I wanted to apologize for the insinuations I made today, and I understand that you might never wish to acknowledge me again. I would deserve the cut."

He pursed his lips and drew closer still. His eyes searched hers, and he nodded. "It is not easy to know the truth about other people."

"But I should not have leaped to a wrong conclusion and accused you of wrongdoing at your own table. You're taking care of your sister as best you can," she told him. "I respect you for that."

And then, because he looked so very surprised by her

words, she stretched up on her toes and dropped a kiss on his cheek the way she would finish an apology to Bennett.

Mamble's skin was warm and slightly rough against her lips, and he smelled of the most divine shaving lotion. He smelled so good that she put her hand on his chest to steady herself as her knees suddenly trembled. Her thoughts about the duke had come full circle and were finally in the right order again though. He was a man worthy of admiration.

He met her gaze, and his eyes were hard. "The other rumors about me *are* true," he said quietly. "I am still a man, Miss Kimble, and right now you are in grave danger of being kissed witless."

Although it was meant as a threat, Gabby found that funny. "I've never been kissed before, witless or otherwise."

The tips of his fingers were suddenly pressing against her middle and pushing her back into the morning room, where he'd left her earlier. He followed, a predatory gleam shining in his eyes. The same look he'd leveled at her in the Windermeres' library. Gabby gulped and nearly stumbled. Perhaps it wasn't wise to put her entire trust in the duke's good nature in *all* matters.

In fact, she might have just made a grave blunder seeking him out. There would be no Lady Windermere to save her today, and Bennett was clearly occupied elsewhere.

The duke's fingers rose and captured her face, tilting it up toward his firmly until she couldn't look anywhere but into his eyes. They were so blue, and he studied her face in a way that made her pulse race with anticipation. Gabby's eyes fluttered closed of their own accord. The next moment, she could feel his breath whisper across her lips, and hers parted as she waited for her first kiss to be delivered.

But his fingers dropped away and the kiss she expected never came.

Gabby opened her eyes to see him some distance away, at the door.

"You deserve someone better than me for your first kiss, Miss Gabriella Kimble," he whispered. "You cannot get what you might wish for from someone like me."

Gabby blinked several times, still off balance from his nearness. "What is it I wish for?"

"A husband," he answered curtly, then he was gone, slipping out the door, leaving an empty space before her and a similar strange emptiness in her soul. She shook her head to clear her confusion and hurried out to the hall again, but Mamble had well and truly vanished this time. Returning to Bennett, no doubt, who would not be at all happy that the duke had almost kissed her, or to know Gabby might have even let him.

Gabby turned about and went to sit at the breakfast table again in a state of utter confusion. She'd almost been kissed today, and to her considerable surprise, she wasn't the least bit sorry it had almost happened. But she was puzzled by her own behavior. Shouldn't she have felt guilty?

Wasn't her great love another man? Lord Brookes. But he'd been far from her mind that morning. In fact, her only thought today had been for the duke, and what he must be going through taking care of his troubled sister.

He had her sympathy and hope that somehow everything would be all right. Yet it was not up to him but Lady Cordelia. It was her life, and Lady Cordelia had to find the will to live it fully or not. Gabby knew from experience that there was little Mamble could do to help his sister than he must already have tried.

When Bennett returned to her alone, solemn, and she was disappointed that the duke was not with him. She had no chance to even see him, as Bennett was keen to be on their way again. He did not look happy with her at all and spoke little on the carriage ride home. But he waited until they were in the privacy of his study, he spoke his mind about her groundless accusations. And the likely repercussions of falling out of favor with so close an acquaintance of Lady Windermere's. A woman she depended on.

Chapter Six

Sebastian lit another candle from the fire because it was late in the day now and he couldn't seem to shake the gloomy mood that had descended over him these past weeks, even with the company of a good friend. "Another drink?"

"Any more and Esme will ring a peal over my head for drunkenness," Windermere murmured. "I'm to escort her to a dinner and then a ball later. Will you be there? At the Foxwood ball?"

"No. I've already sent my apologies."

Windermere frowned to hear the news. "You are in danger of becoming a recluse again. Hiding from society only strengthens the rumors."

"I'm not hiding. I go to my club, and riding each morning, too."

"But I don't see you at dinners or out dancing like you were a few weeks ago. I could always stand another sensible man to talk to between sets or courses."

"Is your wife not enough company for you now?" Sebastian asked, surprised by Windermere's comments. They had gone months before without seeing each other, and he'd never once complained.

"She is but," Windermere said slowly, shifting uncomfortably in his chair, "she's involved herself in a scheme I cannot fully support."

Sebastian stared at his friend in surprise. Windermere and his wife might actually have a disagreement over something at last. It had been all roses and heated looks since the moment they'd married. Sebastian had assumed those two had put any difference of opinion firmly behind them when they'd tied the knot. Apparently not all of them. "What sort of scheme?"

"What was her favorite topic the last time you spoke to her?"

He remembered, and Sebastian heaved a sigh. "Which poor soul is she trying to get leg-shackled now?"

"I would not call Miss Kimble a poor soul. She seems willing enough to make *any* match now."

The mention of Gabby had him shifting in his chair too. "I see. She's still got her heart set on Brookes?"

"Not only Brookes. There's Pendleberry's youngest, Holtby's heir, and Foxwood's middle son being talked of now. It's not right to corner my friends and acquaintances when they call on me at home, and I told her I won't have it again, for all the good that did me. Banished from my own drawing room since. She's even moved the pair in with us."

"Which pair?"

"Bennett and Gabby Kimble," Windermere complained. "Not that I mind Kimble's company, of course, but I would like to have been consulted before the offer was made."

"Quite right," Sebastian agreed. "She should have indeed."

After his talk with Kimble weeks ago, seeking clarity about his intentions toward his ward Gabby and receiving a denial he had any, Sebastian had turned his back on the pair and society at large.

Kimble had also expression concern about Cordelia's situation and his. The fact that Brookes had sought the man out just to warn him not to expect the duke's addresses to Gabby to be sincere or continue had been irritating but nothing but the truth though.

Sebastian had as much interest in marriage as Brookes did. Only Brookes never came out and said so. He'd let women make a fool of themselves over him and enjoy it. Sebastian could not do that to any woman. Not after Cordelia had been so badly disappointed.

No, it was best if he let the gossip subside again and wait for news of Gabby's impending marriage before venturing into society again. It was fortunate he'd made such a decision. He'd avoided running headlong into her when he called on the Windermere's.

Sebastian had thought Gabby too inexperienced to make much of a challenge when first they'd met. She wouldn't be like that for long after Esme's constant influence took hold.

"Esme has taken it upon herself to take the girl under her wing and mold her in her own image. A new wardrobe, hairstyle, escorting her everywhere about Town. Whispering in her ear about things an innocent is likely not supposed to know about before marriage. It's been almost impossible to get my wife's attention these last weeks," Windermere continued on, unaware that his words were causing Sebastian equal parts amusement and concern. Gabby would flex her claws soon, no doubt, and the other gentlemen would fall under her spell. No man in his right mind would hesitate to seduce the young woman if given half the chance.

"I'd put down my foot about it all," Windermere

continued, "but she promises me that Gabby will have a proposal from someone any day now."

Sebastian's stomach did a strange flop. "To whom?"

"Damned if I know or that they'd warn me," he complained. When Sebastian looked up, Windermere was regarding him sternly. "Can you at least promise to drop by tonight's ball? I could use some sensible company."

Sebastian frowned. He didn't feel very sensible right now. In fact, he felt compelled to go rescue Gabby from the man's wife. He had liked Gabby the way she was when they'd met. Optimistic. "You have Kimble. Your wife's cousin. Surely, as guardian, he has the final say on all matters concerning his ward's future."

"Esme can be very persuasive when she wants to be. Kimble is happily going along with everything she wants done out of misplaced gratitude, so far. Yet can you tell me there's nothing better than a conversation with an old friend rather than a new one," Windermere said and then stood abruptly, glancing at his pocket watch and grimacing. "And now I must go back. We're escorting Gabby to a luncheon, where my wife will probably not speak to me for hours. I miss the days when I had her complete attention. I suppose the only way to get her back might be to go along with her scheme to marry off Gabby as quickly as possible."

He left with the shake of his head, leaving Sebastian conflicted. Who would have thought Windermere would be so possessive of his wife's time and attention? His friend had been happily married, content and at ease, only a few weeks ago. But now he was pushed aside, relegated to an afterthought, while his wife helped Gabby snare herself a worthy husband.

Brookes, or someone just like him.

He growled softly, something he'd caught himself doing more of lately. He'd been on edge and was getting worked up over every little thing. He'd even snapped at his valet this morning for taking too long with his shave. Not a good idea when the man had a sharp blade poised at his throat.

Even with Cordelia, he was losing patience. He wanted his sister back, the way she used to be before her season had changed her for the worse.

He leaned back in his chair and closed his eyes, worried suddenly about the changes he might discover in Gabby the next time they met. He growled again, moody, and restless still, and he knew exactly why, of course.

The kitten was out there, sharpening her claws and trying to win the heart of some poor fool, and it could be Brookes that still had her heart.

He'd dreaded reading the newssheet, fearing he'd see an announcement of a marriage in the paper, or overhear gossip at the club to that effect in these past few weeks. At least he assumed she was still trying to throw herself at that unworthy idiot, Brookes, but Esme might have found other, better prospects.

He pressed his head against the back of the chair and suppressed another groan.

"Are you asleep?" Cordelia whispered, and Sebastian snapped open his eyes immediately.

"Just resting my head," he answered, watching her watching *him* from the safety of the doorway. It was so rare that Cordelia came down from her room this early in the afternoon, he didn't know what to say at first. He did not want to have her scurry off with a misplaced comment about his evening plans, not that he had any. "Windermere was here, complaining that his wife is too busy for him."

"That's odd. I thought they were happy."

"Well, I think they are still, but Esme has decided to help Gabby Kimble snare herself a husband for the last few weeks and he's feeling overlooked. He'll get over it once Gabby is safely married off," Sebastian promised, but the last came out as a growl again.

Cordelia edged a little closer. "It's kind of Esme to help her cousin. Gabby seemed nice when she was here."

"I thought so too once."

"Once?" Her brow furrowed. "Don't you think so anymore?"

He shrugged. "I haven't seen her lately."

"Why not?" Cordelia sat down across from him, a look of concern on her face. "Do you not want to see her again?"

"I never said I didn't," he said quickly.

She sighed. "Is *she* why you're always in a bad mood now?"

He smiled quickly. "I am not in a bad mood."

Cordelia nodded. "Yes, you are. You're also bored. I can always tell."

"I'm never bored when you're around," he promised, giving her a reassuring smile he hoped hid his preoccupation with the very idea of other men courting Gabby Kimble. Of Gabby flirting with other men...or her tongue anywhere upon them.

"Yes, you *are*," she claimed, but with a smile on her face. "You always were. You've too much energy to sit around the town house with me like this. You should go out, little brother. See people you like and who like you. Maybe you could dance with Miss Kimble at tonight's ball? I know you enjoyed it the last time."

He narrowed his eyes at her. "How do you know we danced together when I never mentioned doing so?"

"Because you told me you did just now." Cordelia smiled impishly, and a little giggle even escaped her lips. "You never could keep a secret from me when you were a lad. It's in what you *don't* say about the women you meet that gives you away. She made an *impression,* didn't she?"

"That she did," he admitted reluctantly. "But not always in a good way."

"You argued?"

"Perhaps we did," he said, watching Cordelia frown in response to that admission.

Cordelia nodded firmly. "Then you need to talk it out with her."

"We talked." And then he'd almost kissed her. Even now he could still remember the expectation on her upturned face, the gentle scent of her perfume teasing his nostrils, and the certainty that he couldn't pursue the woman for a wife until Cordelia improved.

She had not won over Cordelia that day, but clearly the woman had not been forgotten. He'd not realized how much he'd hoped for that. But his sister had fled from Gabby and that was the end of it. At least, he'd thought so until now.

"You're not happy with the result of your last conversation with her, are you?"

He smiled. He had been pleased that Gabby did not think him a monster, or Cordelia's gaoler either. "I honestly don't know what I feel."

"Ah, then that explains everything," Cordelia replied,

folding her hands in her lap. "You do like her, and not just a little bit, I suspect."

He'd not seen Gabby in weeks. Weeks where he'd prowled the house like an angry bear, wondering if he'd made a mistake by not kissing her. "I like her," he admitted.

"I thought I would hear her name again, but you've not spoken of Gabby since the morning she came."

Sebastian grunted. Although hiding herself away upstairs, lost in her own world, Cordelia had paid attention to what went on in his life. "There is a problem with Gabby Kimble."

"What could that possibly be?"

"She has set her heart on catching herself a fool to marry this season."

"A particular fool, or any fool who thinks to have her?"

"Brookes. Viscount Brookes."

Cordelia made a face. "She is far too smart for that man."

His sister had said not a word about approving of Gabby Kimble after her last visit. "How do you know Gabby is smart?"

"Because *you* must think so." Cordelia winced. "You wouldn't have introduced her to me if she wasn't someone you admired or respected." She smiled quickly. "You used her first name from the very beginning."

"She thought you were my prisoner, Cordie, as many in society do still," he murmured. "She knows better now that she's met you."

Cordelia looked down at her hands. "I'm sorry I didn't make a better impression when we met. Had I known of your interest, I would have tried harder to ignore the flutters in my stomach and stayed."

"You did fine," he assured her. "But she's in love with that fool, Brookes, and that is the end of it. Esme will ensure she marries well."

Cordelia stood. "I'm sorry she's already fallen in love, Sebastian. If she'd met you first, it would have been *you* she fell for. You're ten times the man Brookes could ever be."

"Thank you, sister."

Cordelia frowned suddenly. "I would like to see her again. Here. Tomorrow. You and her guardian can take tea or do whatever men do while we talk again," she announced suddenly. "I promise I won't run away this time."

Cordelia smiled and swept out of the room then, leaving Sebastian stunned by her announcement. She'd never wanted anyone around before. But it seemed discussing Gabby, a woman he admitted he liked, had finally loosened her tongue and eased her mind.

Sebastian breathed a sigh of relief and ran a hand over his face.

If this went well, perhaps Cordelia might invite Gabby and even others for tea in the future.

Feeling a great weight lift from his shoulders, he grinned and stood, his restlessness and bad mood purged by a single conversation with his older sister. Cordelia was intrigued by Gabby. That gave him hope. It was a clear sign that Cordelia would not cut herself off from the world entirely forever.

He wanted to shout with glee, in fact.

But most of all, he wanted to find Gabby and thank her. She might not have done anything on purpose, but because of her, Cordelia would host her very first social engagement since Sebastian had become the duke.

It was definitely cause for celebration, and not just at his club. He wanted to dance.

He wanted to dance with Gabby again.

He rushed upstairs and along to his bedchamber, summoned his valet to change for an evening out at a ball. Lady Foxwood's ball was tonight, and although he'd given his excuses, she would forgive him for having a change of heart at the last moment. He was a duke, and changing his mind was one of the best perks he knew.

Gabby would certainly be there.

His valet was a little rattled by his summons and his impatience to make himself presentable. But it only took an hour before the Duke of Mamble was deemed fit for presentation to society.

It took no time at all to reach the ball and the hostess gushed over his arrival, as expected. He could not outright ask if the Kimbles had arrived already. That would draw unnecessary attention, so he had to mingle first, moving slowly from group to group until he found Lady Windermere at last.

She was delighted to see him. "I so hoped you'd change your mind about tonight."

"Yes, I had a change of heart. Your husband visited me today and nearly got down on his knees to beg me to join him here, claiming you've all but abandoned him."

"Windermere played his part beautifully then," Esme said, grinning.

"His part?"

"He knows how vital the first season can be for a debutant, and I knew if I got a little too busy, he would run to you and complain right on cue. Gabby needs your help again, I'm afraid."

Sebastian froze in utter shock. Windermere had been manipulated by his own wife and had then unknowingly duped *him* as well. The countess had used her husband to lure Sebastian out into society again—and all to help Gabby make a match with someone else.

He did not dare turn straight away to glare at the man's wife, but his mood turned decidedly toward anger. "Is that so?"

"Absolutely," Esme complained with some heat, missing or perhaps ignoring his frosty tone. "It seems one of her friends has also set her heart on capturing Lord Brookes' attention, as well."

"Well, there is no accounting for taste," he bit out.

"Without your fleeting attention, her popularity has plummeted," Esme confessed, drawing even closer. "Despite my best efforts to guide her toward other men, you'll find her determined to remain standing on the sidelines most nights, waiting for Brookes to ask her to dance."

He winced at the picture, a scene he'd witnessed before. "That is unfortunate."

"And also fixable, now that you are here," Esme suggested, brightening suddenly, prodding him with her fan. "Offer to dance with her, and other gentlemen will do the same."

But Sebastian did not want other men to notice Gabby, and he shook his head firmly. "If men like Brookes continue to ignore Gabby Kimble, then that is their loss."

It had been his loss, though, too. Keeping away from Gabby for the last few weeks meant he'd not known of her struggles against a romantic rival. He thought he was glad about it, though.

"Sadly, that is true," Esme murmured, nodding, but it was clear to see she expected him to do something about her popularity still.

If he went to her, others would reconsider her again. But how else was he to talk to Gabby tonight to arrange her visit with Cordelia? He would not have Cordelia disappointed tomorrow. He made himself shrug. "Where might I find your husband?"

"In the card room with my cousin Bennett. When you see him, tell him to come dance with me. I'm feeling peevish," she said, scowling.

"Perhaps he shouldn't come then," Sebastian suggested. Even with the ill use he'd been put to tonight, he did not want to pull his friend away from his pleasures just to potentially have an argument with his peevish wife.

"Oh, he'll come, and running if you repeat my message word for word," she promised with a sly wink.

Sebastian considered her expression for a long moment and decided it was best not to ask what that was all about. Some husbands and wives were said to develop their own private languages.

He ambled from the room as quickly as possible without drawing attention to himself. Windermere and Kimble were just getting up from a table when he entered the room. They both seemed pleased that Sebastian had arrived and in great spirits.

He relayed Esme's message word for word, and Windermere fairly sprinted from the card room to lift his wife's peevish mood.

Sebastian shook his head and Kimble laughed. "Best not to ask, I think," he murmured.

"Yes, it was better for all concerned if we know nothing of what that message really meant to imply," Sebastian agreed.

He turned to Kimble and smiled. "That matter we discussed a few weeks ago...I should like to revisit the idea again. Are you free tomorrow morning?"

"Unfortunately, no," Kimble said, his tone a bit more reserved than the last time they'd met.

"Could you possibly postpone your appointment?"

"Morning calls?" Kimble admitted eventually, and then sighed. "My ward might skin me alive if I deny her the opportunity to talk with her dance partners from tonight."

"Ah," Sebastian said, and then he winced. He'd forgotten that Gabby would be glued to the parlor tomorrow morning, waiting for gentlemen to call upon her.

Although...she had not danced tonight, according to Esme. But she might still find a partner to take the floor within the next hours.

Hmm, how could he prevent her from dancing with anyone else this evening so she could visit Cordelia tomorrow instead? He could approach her to talk and frighten off other gentlemen with a ducal glare, or he could simply abduct her.

He shook his head at both ideas. Such measures surely were not necessary just yet. That smacked of too much desperation.

"I wanted to thank you for the introduction to Lady Cordelia," Kimble said suddenly. "I have wondered how she fared for a very long time."

Sebastian looked at the man sharply. "I was not aware you were acquainted with my sister."

"Ah, she did not tell you how we met, though I suppose we were never formally introduced," Kimble said, and a forgiving smile appeared on his face. "But I could never forget her. She is a remarkably beautiful woman."

"She is," he agreed, and curiosity got the better of him. "Where and when did you first see Cordelia?"

"Here in London, but we were never formally introduced. A lifetime ago, it seems now," he admitted. "She had just come out into society. She was the talk of London from the very first moment."

"Ah," he said slowly. No wonder the man had stared at Cordie for so long when they were introduced. If Kimble had been present during Cordelia's first season, too, then he might actually know more than Sebastian did about that time.

Sebastian cleared his throat. "It was Cordelia who expressed a desire to take tea with Gabby again and have you visit with me. She hopes to make a better impression than the last time you met, I believe," he admitted. "Could you please convey that to your ward, and my desire she accept the invitation if you are both free tomorrow morning?" he asked. "Cordelia hasn't asked anything of me, or to see anyone, since I became duke, and I am loathe to disappoint her in this matter."

Kimble froze for a long moment, but then he nodded. "Well, in that case. We'd be honored to visit you both tomorrow. It won't be hard to convince Gabby to disappoint any suitors who might call tomorrow. She'll want to come and make things right."

Chapter Seven

As GABBY STOOD on the sidelines of yet another ball, her heart continued to sink through the floor. The room was a sea of brightly colored gowns, elegant hairstyles, and sparkling jewelry but she felt apart from the merriment. The other debutants seemed to have all found their feet. They belong here, but Gabby was no longer certain she could ever feel the same.

She experienced a pang of envy as she watched the other ladies twirl and glide by on the arms of their handsome partners, wishing she might be dancing with her suitor...if she had one. However, many of those women had greater dowries than hers, so it was to be expected that they might be pursued by men in need of funds.

But were all of society's gentlemen so dim? Did they not value a woman with intelligence too?

Gabby didn't let her disappointment show, nor dare run to find her cousin or Lady Windermere, to bolster her declining spirits. No, she put on a polite smile and circled the dance floor with Daisy and observed the proceedings just as she had for weeks.

Couples moved around them, laughing, and chatting, and she wondered what it would be like to be the center of someone's attention like that. For a while, she'd believed she'd *had* a man's attention that way, but then he had gone away.

Her eyes were drawn as they often were to Lord Brookes, but now when she looked at his ever-present smile, she distrusted the emotion behind it. He had singled out Justine for attention this week, dancing with her and promenading the room with her.

Yet last week it had been another debutant entirely who had captivated his attention.

Her eyes were drawn to Justine's smiling face and sighed. She appeared to be having a marvelous time despite claiming she had no interest in Lord Brookes from the start.

Gabby had never managed to dance even once with Brookes and had given up hope a few nights ago. What was there about him that had drawn her notice in the first place? Was it only that he was handsome, and always smiling? Was there anything of substance underneath that smile to attach her feelings to?

And Justine, dancing with Lord Brookes, seemed to bask in his company. When the set ended, Justine and Brookes returned to her sister's side. They chatted for a few moments and then Brookes went away. Justine fanned her face, while her sister whispered in her ear.

Although Gabby tried to catch her eye several times, Justine never once looked their way or moved to join them. She hadn't since the first night Brookes had singled her out, too.

Daisy suddenly dug her elbow into Gabby's side. "Did you hear that?"

"What?"

"He's here," Daisy whispered excitedly. "The Duke of Mamble is here."

Gabby's stomach lurched and she looked around, but she did not see him in the ballroom.

A duke had almost kissed her.

A man she had wronged from the start. She had apologized and believed herself forgiven, but she had not seen him again since that day. She might have imagined he'd gone back to the country, but Lady Windermere and her husband spoke of his activities in London often.

And Gabby had foolishly looked for him the past weeks and wondered how he fared, and how his sister was getting on, too.

Yet wasn't it foolish to long to see the duke again? Just as ridiculous as her preoccupation with Lord Brookes had been. Neither man would consider her for their wife.

But it had been as clear as the tip of her nose that the Duke of Mamble found her attractive, which was more than she could say of Brookes' fleeting interest. An almost-kiss was a significant step up from mouthing empty pleasantries, and that kiss might have happened if she wasn't so young and inexperienced of men.

Perhaps, too, it was her lack of dowry that discouraged a pursuit. Gabby didn't put much stock in Lady Windermere's claim that their distant relationship gave her a significant advantage over other debutants and increased her chances of making a great match this season.

Yet after all these weeks in society, Gabby still clung to hope that some man would choose her for herself. However, when Mamble had vanished from society, no one had asked her to dance with them again. She was beginning to feel like a pariah, or a plain and dull wallflower. She knew that her cousin was hoping for a good match and espoused patience. But the last thing Gabby wanted was to burden Bennett with the expense of a second season.

But what more could she do to stand out from the crowd than she'd done already? She had no great talent for music; she was pretty but not stunning like Lady Cordelia was.

As she stood there, lost in her thoughts, a voice interrupted her reverie. "Excuse me, Miss Kimble. May I have this dance?"

Gabby looked up to see Mamble, tall and devastatingly handsome, standing before her again, a charming smile on his lips. She blinked in surprise that he would even bother to approach her.

Yet without a second thought, Gabby placed her hand in his, and they moved onto the dance floor together. As they began to dance the waltz in silence, Gabby felt a glimmer of foolish hope lighten her heart. Maybe, just maybe, tonight would be different, and the night her fortunes changed again for the better, thanks solely to the duke.

She glanced beyond his shoulder and suddenly felt self-conscious in his arms that so many people stared at them already. They were probably wondering why he'd chosen to dance with her out of all others. She'd like to know that, as well.

"Ignore them," he whispered.

She would if she didn't feel picked apart by every eye. "Where have you been?"

"Home," he whispered, and her stomach lurched in dread.

She wet her lips to whisper back, "I trust your sister remains in good health."

"Cordelia could actually be improving," he whispered back. He squeezed her hand a little more firmly, and then softened his grip again.

"That is good news." Gabby squeezed his hand back to express her relief. "I was afraid for a moment she might be worse because of me."

"She wants to see you. Tomorrow morning," Mamble confessed.

"I should love to see her, too," Gabby said, dropping her eyes to his broad expanse of chest because her cheeks were growing warm, thanks to his cologne filling her lungs again. "I feared our presence might have frightened her the last time."

Mamble tightened his grip on her fingers. "Will you come?"

"For breakfast?"

"No, a little later. Cordelia wishes you to join her for tea midmorning. You can bring your guardian."

Gabby immediately realized the timing was problematic. The morning after a ball was a crucial time for a debutant. She might have gentlemen call on her at home—except none but the duke had asked her to dance so far tonight.

In recent weeks, too, the number of morning callers had dwindled from the crush the duke's attention had first instigated to none, though. Even moving to stay with Lady Windermere had not improved the situation.

Tomorrow could be more of the same. Gabby waiting for hours, and she didn't want to do that again. Besides, it might only be the duke calling on her tomorrow, anyway. She did want to see him, and talk to his sister, too. Cordelia would not come to her.

"I will be pleased to call on your sister," she promised. "I would like that very much."

"Good," he said firmly, and she was pulled in a little closer to his chest. "There will be a formal invitation waiting by the time you return home."

"We are staying with Lady Windermere," she said quickly, in case he hadn't heard the news.

"I already knew that," he said with a wink.

Gabby tried to return a smile that she hoped did not reveal how pleased she was that he knew where to find her. Being in the duke's arms made her feel better. She was deeply interested in nurturing a friendship with his shy sister, even if the duke did not want her for anything else.

Their dance was ending, and her time with Mamble was almost over. He spun her quickly for the final turns, let her go, and then stepped back to bow deeply to her.

Gabby curtsied, and then straightened to clap along with everyone else. But her dance with the duke had gone so quickly that she was disappointed it was already over. Might he linger at her side tonight, or would he flee like he had the last time they danced together?

Mamble moved closer, and his fingers settled briefly at the small of her back. "To Miss Ellis or to your cousin?" he enquired.

"To Miss Ellis, if you please," she whispered back, pleased that he remembered the name of her friend and fighting a shiver.

He accompanied her all the way to Daisy's side and even spoke with her for a few minutes. But as she'd feared, he took his leave of her too soon, and then of the ballroom entirely.

"My word," Daisy said, fanning herself. "How are you still standing?"

"I beg your pardon?" Gabby asked, dragging her eyes away from the distant doorway.

"The way Mamble looked at you tonight was almost indecent," Daisy whispered. "You will be the talk of the *ton* tomorrow."

"He just looks at me like he does anyone else," Gabby said, shrugging away her accusation.

"No, my dear," Daisy chided. "That is how a man who *wants* should look at a woman dancing in his arms."

"There is nothing like that between us," she whispered, embarrassed by Daisy's suspicions.

"Well, that is sad, because it's clear he is as interested in you as you are in him."

"In his sister," she said quickly. "I have been invited to take tea with Lady Cordelia tomorrow morning."

"If I were you, I would find a way to *take* anything the duke might put in front of you tomorrow, too," Daisy whispered, and then chuckled. "Oh, that was wicked of me, wasn't it? I should add *make sure he'll marry you first*, of course, before too much excitement happens between you."

Gabby gaped. When Justine was not around, Daisy became more outspoken and blunt and had revealed the startling fact that she was no sheltered young miss, either. She knew a lot more about the behavior of amorous men and women than Gabby had ever suspected could exist.

Despite Daisy's blunt honesty, Gabby still had not admitted that she'd almost been kissed by the Duke of

Mamble. Gabby leaned close to whisper in Daisy's ear, "What would be considered too much?"

"A kiss, a close embrace, a little panting," Daisy said with a laugh. "But if it feels right..."

"Feels right?"

Every moment with Mamble had felt wonderful. She recalled with perfect clarity how he'd almost kissed her. She'd wanted his lips on hers. She might have let him get all the way to a little panting, too. But that had been long after her foolish declaration to him about admiring Lord Brookes.

She had not understood at the time how she could have felt that way about the duke if she was intent on catching Lord Brookes' eye. Why she'd not been more concerned about her virtue around the duke? Now she was no longer torn over her initial attraction to the two men though. However, she'd no idea if it could be more.

Mamble, a man who made her decidedly unsettled, was a duke and so far above her she didn't truly imagine he could have any serious interest. He'd even told her so.

Brookes was a well-to-do viscount, but not as rich as the duke must surely be. He might have always intended to marry a woman who brought riches to his pocket. Justine's dowry was greater than Gabby's.

Gabby turned to find her friend in the crowd. Justine had claimed disinterest in Brookes, but there she was, standing right beside him again and smiling up at him.

"Daisy, are we sure Justine is not in love with anyone?" Gabby asked, finally willing to consider the possibility Justine had not been truthful about ambitions for matrimony.

"She never said so to me," Daisy whispered back. "But

then she was always more your friend than mine. Why do you ask?"

"It's probably nothing. Just my imagination getting the worst of me," Gabby promised.

"Best to turn your mind to being whatever the Duke of Mamble might desire instead," Daisy suggested before being pulled away to dance with a friend of her glowering guardian's.

Gabby still had no dance partners and moved back to her cousin Bennett's side, but she kept an eye on Justine. The woman still ignored her. Had Gabby been entirely wrong about their friendship surviving the rigors of the season? Would they even get to the end of it and still be speaking?

She dropped her eyes to her fingers, wishing the duke had stayed a little longer to distract her. Not because he was rich and powerful, but because he was the only man she'd met who she felt spoke to her as if her opinion mattered.

A duke could do largely as he pleased, and that could also extend to making a marriage to someone without a vast dowry other men might insist upon. Perhaps Daisy had the right of it. Perhaps she ought to have aimed a little higher in her expectations.

Of all the balls she'd known Mamble to have attended in recent weeks, he'd only danced with a few ladies. Herself, and older married friends of his. Gabby had danced with Mamble twice but had not taken the time to appreciate the experiences. Would it be weeks before they might dance together again?

Brookes had done nothing to earn or keep her admiration. It had been Gabby pursuing the idea of him as a husband all along, and as she saw Justine laugh and attach herself to the viscount's arm, she acknowledged she might have made a miscalculation.

Bennett nudged her. "Why so great a sigh?"

She looked up at her cousin. Bennett believed she would make a good match. But there was no one beside the duke that appealed to her. "I think I should like to go home early."

"Oh? Why?"

"I just...I think I have a headache coming on," she fibbed, hoping that was explanation enough to obtain his agreement. Bennett had quite enjoyed the balls they'd been attending lately. He'd earned his own string of feminine admirers too. He liked to dance and flirt and do all the things bachelors could to win over feminine hearts. Though he had not shown particular interest in any one woman so far.

Bennett slowly nodded. "Very well, we can leave after you've said good night to Daisy and told Lady Windermere. You've thrown yourself into the season with vigor, but perhaps you ought to be more selective of the invitations you accept."

"Yes, perhaps I should," she promised. She did not tell Bennett yet that she was expecting to find an invitation to join the duke's sister for tea tomorrow, or that she was eager to accept it. He would find out for himself soon enough and would most likely agree that such an invitation could not possibly be declined.

She wanted to see Cordelia and the Duke of Mamble again very much.

Chapter Eight

Sebastian paused before the drawing room doors the next day and cautiously glanced inside, curious to know what he'd find. Cordelia had been up at first light, flitting about the house, and was now arranging flowers for her first ever at-home since he'd inherited his title.

It was obvious she was nervous.

He was too.

If today went well, it might mean many more intimate gatherings with other women could take place in his home. If it went badly, Cordelia might never recover her confidence, and he would not see Gabby again, most likely.

He did not want that.

He affected a nonchalant air, though, as he sauntered into the room and clapped his hands together to get his sister's attention. Today had to go well. "Ready?"

"Not quite," Cordelia warned, adjusting a little figurine on the mantel a quarter turn. She was looking remarkably elegant today. Her rose-pink modest gown was simple enough for the occasion of meeting a potential new friend, while reminding everyone of her position in society. Her hair was upswept in an older style she'd favored, and there was even a hint of color on her cheeks again. "There now. That has bothered me for a very long time."

He laughed softly. "Has it now?"

"Indeed. Mother never let me change anything," Cordelia confided, with a rueful laugh.

"Well, she's not here to stop you doing anything anymore," he promised before dropping a kiss on her brow for added reassurance. "You can go on making changes if you like. This is your home."

"I know, and I want everything to go perfectly today," Cordelia announced, her grin expanding as she surveyed her realm.

"If there's any lack, it will not be on your part," he promised, intrigued by her high expectations for the morning.

Gabby was something of a mystery still, but he could hardly expect her to be disappointed at being received by a duke's beloved sister for a second time.

The knocker sounded, and he turned about, automatically straightening his cravat and pulling down his waistcoat. He was nervous about seeing Gabby, and about what might have happened after he'd left the ball last night. Just how many undeserving swains had approached Gabby to dance because of his renewed attentions this time?

Had Brookes sought her out?

The man she'd wanted to wed when they had first met.

He forced his uncertainty aside as the butler announced the Kimbles, and his heart did the tiniest of flips at the sight of Gabby gliding gracefully into the room.

She was simply dressed for her morning call. Her dark hair was pinned at the back of her neck, but a few stray curls had escaped to curl around her face and slender throat. He wanted to brush them back, so he had an unobstructed view of her skin.

Pleasantries were exchanged, the weather commented upon, and then Cordelia coughed. He turned to her in alarm, but she only smiled. "You are excused, brother."

He gaped a moment before remembering he'd summoned Kimble to discuss Gabby with him in private. "Indeed. Come along, Kimble. Let's not bore the ladies with our business."

"We would not be bored by you, your grace," Gabby answered. "But we ladies have important matters to discuss."

He inclined his head, secretly pleased with her response. She was smart and no wilting wallflower. But the priority today was Cordelia.

Kimble seemed to make a point to bid Cordelia adieu.

In the hall, he caught Kimble's eye. "I appreciate you both coming."

"Gabby was excited by the invitation," Kimble began. "She has been worried she might have upset your sister. She is very keen to know your sister better and make amends for her mistake," Kimble said. "I'm sure you must understand why."

Sebastian frowned at the man. "I don't follow you, I'm afraid?"

"Her father," Kimble said, and then sighed. "Ah, Esme didn't tell you how I came to be Gabby's guardian then."

He'd not truly questioned Esme about her cousin for fear the woman might have read too much into his enquiries. "What about her father?" he asked.

"On the surface, Maxwell Kimble was a proud and happy man. Married, with a child he adored. Respected by all. But there were times when a black melancholy would descend over him. When his wife died, those black periods recurred with greater frequency."

"Gabby knew about it?" Sebastian glanced back to the open doorway and beyond, where Gabby now sat with Cordelia.

"Gabby saw it all, until the end," Kimble explained.

Sebastian's stomach pitted and rolled. "How did her father die?"

Kimble held up one hand. "In his sleep, during a rare happy period in his life."

Sebastian exhaled in relief. But he didn't want Gabby exposed to the ongoing tragedy that was his sister's withdrawal from the world. He wet his lips. "Perhaps encouraging my sister and your ward toward friendship was not a good idea."

"Not at all. They are utterly different people and circumstances. Gabby likes Cordelia very much. I saw that from the start, and once she makes up her mind to befriend someone, there is no stopping her from giving them her heart and loyalty," Kimble explained, one brow raised. "Leave the ladies to it. They will either get along or they will not."

"Yes, true," he said as he studied Kimble. "I must say you seem to have taken on the role of guardian very well. I can't imagine it was easy to suddenly have the responsibility of a young cousin. For me, it was a struggle with my older sisters when I inherited. Suddenly being in charge of both."

"I like to think of it as I've been blessed. Gabby largely takes care of herself, and she has always enjoyed running my household. The only time I've seen her truly nervous was the morning you came to call after your first dance."

Sebastian raised a brow at that. "Was my reputation so fearsome?"

"It's always the unknown that unsettles her. You are a duke, and I wonder what you really want with her even now. She has only a small dowry, a bit of land, and a tenuous connection to Lady Windermere."

"Indeed," Sebastian agreed. He gestured for Kimble to take a seat close beside the fire. "I have been thinking about what you said to me, about planning for the future."

"It is always a good idea," Kimble murmured. "Especially for a man in your exalted position."

"You are not the only one to suggest that lately," he said bluntly. "I would like us to come to an understanding."

Kimble studied him for a long moment. "No."

Sebastian was taken by surprise by the firmly voiced decline. "You don't even know what I was going to ask."

Kimble pursed his lips. "It is readily apparent that despite your invitation to me, it is Gabby who's here to be approved of. I won't have her led on like this."

Sebastian shifted in his chair. "I can't, *won't*, commit myself to any woman who thinks ill of my sister."

"Gabby is the last person who would do that," Kimble said, eyes narrowing suddenly. "But it is you who perhaps thinks the worst of my ward."

Sebastian tapped the arm of his chair before he spoke. "People have been unkind about Cordelia."

"To you as well, painting you as a tyrant. Her gaoler. Calling you cruel," Kimble suggested.

"I will admit that hurts," he said.

"You are a duke. The ill-informed should never bother you," the man chided.

Sebastian studied Kimble again. "If I may ask, how old are you?"

"Older than I look," he said with a shrug. "Older than your sister by at least a year, I think."

"Oh," he said, noticing that Kimble brought up Cordelia again. She had become a point of reference in all their conversations.

"I want her to be happy. It is vital to me that my sister never again feels herself lacking. My parents treated her as chattel." Sebastian pursed his lips. "And I know what I want now, but I'm not sure of your wards interests."

The man frowned. "Why would Gabby, or any woman, not be interested in becoming a duchess?"

"In *me*," he countered. "As you surely must know, she has long had her heart set on another."

Kimble's eyes widened. "Who?"

Sebastian winced. "I'd rather not say. But you can imagine it makes a man hesitate."

"Yes, indeed it would," Kimble agreed, and then stood up to pace the room. Sebastian left him to it. Kimble knew his ward far better than he did yet. But he did not know about her infatuation with Viscount Brookes, it seemed.

Kimble suddenly spun around to face Sebastian. "What are your intentions toward my ward?"

"Marriage in the end, but only if her heart is not otherwise engaged."

"A sensible precaution," Kimble agreed, nodding. "Very well, you have my blessing for a pursuit but...disgrace her, and you will live to regret it."

Sebastian stood. "I am a man of my word, but I do not appreciate threats."

A woman's piercing scream echoed through the house.

Kimble spun around. "Cordelia?"

The man sprinted for the drawing room and left Sebastian to follow.

When Sebastian arrived, Kimble was on his knees beside Cordelia, where she lay across the couch.

Gabby seemed equally as lifeless, bent awkwardly over the arm of her chair. Sebastian went to her first, touching her face and holding a finger under her nose to check for the breath of life. "Gabby?"

Gabby squinted at him through one eye. "Did you think I was dead?"

"What?"

"Dead? Did you believe us murdered?"

He took a step back and glanced across at Cordie, who seemed not to have moved from her prone position. Kimble had his head bowed over her still. "Of course not."

"Well, I damn well did," Kimble cursed, climbing to his feet and jerking Cordelia upright. "You must never to do that again!"

Cordie put her hand on Kimble's arm, and Sebastian suddenly realized the man was trembling—with rage. Or was it fear? "I asked her to act with me. It was my idea to shriek. I had no idea the sound would travel to you."

Sebastian put his hand over his heart, which still raced from the fright he'd just suffered. "Kimble, I do apologize for the misunderstanding."

Kimble's gaze never left Cordelia's face. "Would you care to explain?" he growled.

"Forgive my sister, Kimble. When she was a girl, she

professed an interest in treading the boards. She once claimed she could act out a death scene better than those at the theater. My parents, of course, forbid her those little theatrics."

"It's only a harmless little play, Bennett," Gabby whispered.

To Sebastian's surprise, Cordelia continued to whisper to Kimble, and even ran her hand up his arm in a soothing gesture.

Finally, Kimble nodded.

Gabby drew closer. "He did not take that well."

Sebastian glanced down at her. "Neither did I. I've just lost five years of my life out of fright, thinking I'd lost you," he warned. "She was horribly convincing."

She smiled brightly, though. "Horribly?"

"Hmm, well yes," he admitted. He glanced across the room to his sister. "You chose today of all days to dust off another forbidden desire of yours?" he called out.

Cordelia glanced his way and smiled, but her hand remained on Kimble's arm. "I wanted to run away from home once, too. I might still do that for the right reason."

Sebastian laughed at the hollow threat.

Kimble's back stiffened, though, and he mumbled something to Cordelia that Sebastian couldn't hear.

Sebastian regarded the pair through narrowed eyes. Something was going on between Cordelia and Kimble right under his nose...or had gone on before. "It would be best if you and Gabby continued your acting another day."

"I'd like that," Gabby gushed. "We could add others later, too. My good friend Miss Ellis would love to join us for a little play. She often takes the male grumpy roles very well, although Bennett would be a better choice right now, don't you think?"

Cordelia frowned at the mention of including others but did not immediately decline the idea of enlarging their group.

"So, it is settled then," he said, clapping his hands together. "There will be acting, but could we not reenact death scenes again?"

Cordelia crossed the room and kissed his cheek. "No death scenes for at least a month to give poor Sebastian's nerves time to prepare."

"And Mr. Kimble's, too. Thank you for your consideration, sister dear." He glanced at his guests. "Well, this has been an eventful morning."

"Indeed," Kimble murmured.

Although the last thing he wanted was for Gabby to leave, he didn't want to press his luck with Cordelia's anxiety. His sister was changing in her company, though and so rapidly, he didn't want anything to go wrong.

"The morning visit isn't over yet, *little* brother" Cordelia said firmly.

Sebastian was surprised but pleased by her asserting her authority over him. "Well, then, we gentlemen should leave you to plan out the next shock for us in secrecy, I suppose," he said, scratching his head.

Cordelia laughed, a sound he'd not heard in a very long time. "Oh, why don't you both join us, Sebastian? I'm sure you've said all you needed to Mr. Kimble this morning."

"Yes, please join us, your grace, and cousin," Gabby agreed, smiling at them in a way that warmed Sebastian's heart to be included.

"All right," he promised, watching as Cordelia approached Kimble again and asked him a question about his time in Town.

"I like her," Gabby whispered, sneaking up to stand close. "She's so funny."

"She used to be," he murmured, keeping an eye on Cordelia and Kimble a moment longer, but then he turned to Gabby. "She's more herself around you than with others who have known her for years."

"Perhaps it is because I know no different?"

"That could be true," he agreed, but it did not explain Bennett Kimble, or Cordie touching his arm, which she was already doing again. He could put a stop to it, but he had noticed it was only Cordelia touching the fellow, not the other way round. "Or it could simply be because you are entirely likable."

"That is not it," Gabby countered with a laugh. "If I was entirely likable, I'd have gentlemen eating out of my hand this season."

He didn't want to ask, but he couldn't stop himself. "No luck with Brookes, then?"

"No." Her expression grew sour. "It seems I have a rival for his affections, and one that I never expected, too."

"I'm sorry to hear that. What will you do?"

Gabby shrugged. "What *can* I do? I cannot make anyone love me."

Sebastian bit his lip. Gabby was easy to love. Brookes was an even greater fool than Sebastian had believed. "You could always begin a nasty rumor about your rival."

"Tempting, except that I liked her very much," Gabby protested.

"Ah, well, if you were desperate for a marriage with him, you could always seduce him?"

She looked up at him steadily. "I would not do that with him or anyone just to have a ring on my finger."

"No?" Sebastian felt a smile twitch his lips. "Recently, I've given thought to the merits of abduction and seduction."

Gabby laughed. "Have you?"

"It would be a way to circumvent a rival and secure the match of our dreams."

Gabby's face clouded with worry. "Perhaps it might, if I were desperate."

"And you're not?"

"I don't think so," she said, looking up with a quick smile. "I wouldn't want to force a man into a marriage with me. I'd like him to like me. For myself."

"I'm glad to hear it." He glanced up and noticed Cordelia and Kimble had moved toward the front of the house and were standing very close with their back toward them, talking quietly together. "But I'm sure it wouldn't be a hardship to be married to you."

He sensed rather than saw Gabby take a tiny step toward him. "You're too kind," she whispered.

"And you are too tempting for your own good," he admitted, glancing her way—and then, unwisely perhaps, given they were not alone, he stole a quick, soundless kiss.

When he lifted his head, Gabby was rather pink in the face, but she did not chide him for taking liberties. In fact, she was watching him rather closely now, but then her gaze widened and flew to the far side of the room, where her guardian stood.

"They are a little distracted right now." Sebastian cleared

his throat. "Could I tempt you to something else, Miss Kimble?"

She gasped; her face turning a brighter shade of pink.

"Tea but in the library," he suggested with a smile. "I hear you are a great reader."

"From whom?"

"Lady Windermere mentioned your fondness for the written word. I'm surprised I never heard you speak of it before."

"It is not wise to mention intelligence when hoping for a husband," Gabby admitted sheepishly.

"That depends on whom you tell," he answered with a wider smile. He faced the pair across the room. "Mr. Kimble, Cordelia. I've promised to show Miss Kimble our library. We will be just over there taking tea instead."

Kimble nodded. "We'll join you in a moment."

Cordelia agreed.

Together, Gabby and Sebastian slipped from the room.

He leaned down. "I think we could have slipped away without even telling them and not be noticed."

"I think you may be right," Gabby agreed, glancing over her shoulder. "I've never known Bennett to be so smitten by a lady before."

"They have history," Sebastian warned. "History I knew nothing about, I might add."

"He was here for her season," Gabby whispered back.

"What else did he say about her?"

"Nothing. He said nothing at all. That's why it's so obvious they were involved somehow once."

Sebastian grunted. "As much as I respect your guardian, I don't believe my father would have approved of the connection then. The expectations for my sister's season were unreasonably high."

Gabby turned on him suddenly. "Would you have approved of him if it had been *your* decision?"

"I learned young to stay out of the way of my older sisters'. I would not have stood in their way then," he promised, placing his hand. "Cordelia has free choice in all things now, I assure you."

Gabby grinned. "You're a romantic at heart."

He drew closer to Gabby. "I know it is unusual among the *ton*, but I have always believed in love before money or titles when choosing a spouse."

She was so close, and he reached out and allowed his hand to skim her hip and then caress up to her waist and back again. Gabby's eyes widened, but she kept her gaze on him. Her stare was direct, but not afraid.

Sebastian moved one step closer to give her derriere a gentle squeeze. Gabby jolted, but she never looked away from him once. In her eyes now was a glimpse of excitement and newly awakened desire. He caressed her bottom a little more, and her lips parted with a soft moan.

He withdrew his hand quickly as Kimble and Cordelia swept into the room.

When Gabby stated outright that she'd given up her pursuit of Brookes, she'd find herself on the receiving end of a much more ardent pursuit from him. But she had not yet. He would wait until her feelings about his rival were expressed more clearly.

He turned his attention to Kimble and Cordelia. They made a handsome pair, but he would not involve himself in their affair—if such a thing was even the case. Cordelia had never taken well to impertinent questions from her younger brother. And Kimble, well he was turning out to be full of surprises, but he was a man who seemed to keep secrets well.

Cordelia announced she'd ring for tea and turned away, Kimble following her like a string joined them together.

He smiled to himself as hope stirred in his heart for a brighter future for his older sister, too. She deserved all the happiness the world had to offer.

Then Sebastian jolted as his bottom was pinched.

It was brief, and he turned quickly to look at Gabby over his shoulder. She held a book in one hand and her eyes were wide on the pages, but nothing else in her expression hinted she'd done anything out of the ordinary.

Yet, he hadn't imagined it.

Gabby had made a bold move toward him—and it made his pulse race with wicked anticipation for future encounters.

She walked past him, book in hand, but a nervous giggle escaped as she hurried to another bookshelf. Sebastian followed, drawn to follow a woman whose good opinion and laughter he craved more and more each day.

"I could spend years trying to read all of these," she murmured, glancing at him over her shoulder.

She could too, but only if Sebastian might have her whole heart in return.

Chapter Nine

"I cannot bear this," Gabby complained to Daisy as they stood on the sidelines at yet another ball. Gabby had been dancing all night for a change, and this was her only free set of the evening to speak with Daisy at any great length.

News had spread about her second visit to Lady Cordelia, and people regarded her with greater curiosity now. Everyone wanted to know about Lady Cordelia and her situation and Gabby discovered she had an unsettling number of new female friends. Aside from confirming Cordelia's good health and freedom, Gabby refused to reveal anything more personal than that.

Lady Windermere and a few other important women had looked upon her approvingly from nearby, too, as they heard her dismiss any outrageous claim made against the Duke of Mamble as evil hearsay and outright slander.

And then, one by one, the gentlemen she'd danced with at previous balls had drawn closer, too. First Lord Triscot, then Lord Paul Holtby, and even Lord Henry Foxwood, too, had asked her to dance with them.

As the evening wore on, Gabby began to suspect she'd passed some kind of test and was now fully approved by the *ton*. A pity the Duke of Mamble was not here to see it and enjoy the night with her, though.

Daisy leaned close. "She has forgotten us."

"But she was our first friend in London, besides each other, of course. What did we do to turn her away from our company?"

"I don't know," Daisy said, worrying her lip.

"Well, I cannot spend the rest of the season wondering about that. Can you?"

"I don't think you'll ever let me forget," Daisy teased. "But, no, I agree. I would like an answer, too."

It was an irritation to Gabby that a perfectly nice young woman was giving them both the cold shoulder for no good reason. Justine had been their friend and confidant. It was an uncomfortable sensation to see her ignore them, and they could hardly avoid running into each other. They were always attending the same events; they shared mutual acquaintances and mutual goals of finding a husband this season. There had to be a good reason for why things had changed.

Gabby squared her shoulders. "Let's get this done now, tonight."

"All right, but please, let's not make it too obvious what we're doing," Daisy pleaded, looking about the room. She hooked her arm through Gabby's. "I don't need to give my guardian another reason to scowl at me."

"Why was he scowling tonight?" Gabby asked.

"I may have mentioned I purchased silk stockings today," Daisy said with a careless shrug.

"He has never liked it when you spend your allowance," Gabby noted, patting her hand.

"It wasn't that I spent the money, but that I showed him I was wearing my purchase tonight," Daisy replied, and then she laughed wickedly. "His eyes rolled toward the ceiling so fast, I thought he might have fainted clean away for a moment. He's been scowling ever since."

"I wish I had been there," Gabby said, imagining such a scene.

"It was a moment I will not forget for the rest of my life," Daisy promised.

They circulated through the room, speaking to anyone with whom they had an acquaintance, and eventually found Justine and her sister more or less alone.

Gabby cleared her throat a few times until the pair looked over their shoulders. "Good evening, Justine. Lady Whitlow."

The older woman inclined her head, but Justine stiffened when her sister moved immediately away. She smiled at them, but it contained none of the warmth of days gone by. "Good evening, Miss Kimble. Miss Ellis."

"It is lovely to see you again, Justine," Daisy gushed. "What a wonderful evening it is."

"Indeed, it *has* been wonderful, *Miss Ellis*," Justine said firmly. Her smile remained in place as she said it, but her eyes traveled the room as if she was bored or looking for an escape.

Gabby wet her lips. "We are so glad you were invited tonight."

"Why would I not attend this ball?" Justine asked, giving Gabby a pointed stare. "My sister is a viscountess while you have a tenuous connection to the ton at best. Besides, I love to dance."

"You are very graceful," Gabby said, because it was true, and then drew closer to Justine. "Justine, is something the matter?"

Justine's face froze, and her smile grew even more rigid. "Nothing has changed for me. I am enjoying the delights of the season as much as any debutant. I have been much engaged elsewhere."

"Too busy to talk to us even at balls such as this? You never speak to us anymore. Not like you used to."

Justine stared at them both for a moment and then glanced behind her. She nodded as if answering someone, and then turned back. "I'm afraid you must excuse me."

"But Justine," Daisy began. "We..."

"You would do well to prepare yourself for further disappointment," Justine warned with a nod.

Well, *former* friend, it seemed now. Justine had not even tried to pretend they were still friends.

Gabby sighed as Justine returned to her sister, and the woman whispered in her ear before leading her away. They went immediately to talk with Lord Brookes, and after a few moments, Justine threw them a smug smirk that she had been the one who had claimed Lord Brookes' attention rather than Gabby.

Daisy understood that look, too, and cursed softly. "The nerve of taunting you. I bet she planned to steal Lord Brookes from you all along, and her sister helped her do it."

Weeks ago, the threat of a rival would have bothered Gabby a great deal more. Tonight, all she felt was a great sadness pressing upon her heart. If Justine had even hinted that her preference for a husband had changed, things could have been so different today. She would like to think they might have remained friends even if Justine had captured Lord Brookes heart. Gabby would never begrudge a friend their one true love, if that is what Justine felt for the viscount now.

Or perhaps she merely wanted a title. Something Gabby wanted a husband for.

She had wanted someone to love more than anything, and for them to love her back.

But suddenly Gabby saw the Duke of Mamble standing across the room at last, watching her, and her concern about Justine evaporated. A sense of profound relief and excitement filled her to see the duke finally appear at another ball. She had never once misunderstood *that* man's interest in her. She knew, bone deep, that he was not toying with her affections because he was bored.

He wanted her. Just her.

There had been a promise in his eyes from the start.

She wet her lips. "Daisy, I have to tell you something important."

"What is it?" Daisy whispered, a worried frown appearing on her face.

"I don't actually admire Lord Brookes as much as I once thought I did," Gabby admitted, blushing as the duke's continued stare made her long to cross the room to talk to him. "I'm not in the least bothered by Justine setting her cap for him."

"I'm very pleased to hear it," Daisy whispered. "It is not healthy for women to compete for the attentions of the same man, especially good friends."

"I agree, which is why I want to ask you outright who you favor. You've never even hinted, and I can't bear to lose another friend so dear to me."

"You'll never lose me over a man," Daisy began, hugging

her arm, but then glanced behind her. Eventually, she shook her head. "That is to say that I don't know what I feel about *any* gentleman I've met in London yet, so there is no rivalry between us."

"So, you've not set your heart on winning a titled husband this season?"

"I'd never say never," Daisy answered after a long moment, and then looked up at her, horrified. "Why? Please don't say you admire my guardian! As a guardian, he is terrible, but as a husband he'd be utterly impossible."

"No, of course not him. He's much too stern for anyone who likes to laugh," she said, but then Gabby took a deep breath. "Would you ever want to become a duchess?"

"Me? A duchess? No." But then a sly smile curved Daisy's lips, and she looked over at Mamble, who was still watching them from afar still and making no attempt to hide his interest tonight. "But I suspect *you* might be."

Gabby bit her lip to hide the telling smile she struggled against as she admired Mamble in return. She was overwhelmed by how she felt about him now. This was not some girlish infatuation that had taken her over. It was more subtle than that, and far more compelling. Something would happen between them. It was only a matter of time.

She glanced in the Viscount's direction once more, briefly, and confirmed the lure of him was utterly gone from her being and shook her head. She locked her eyes on Mamble. She knew which gentleman she preferred now. Which man she'd like to be seduced by, too. "I like the duke very much."

Daisy's hands flew to cover her lips. "Then what are you doing still standing here with me for? Go get him."

She would love to do just that—except Mamble had turned away and was heading out of the ballroom. He couldn't be leaving!

Fearing he'd misunderstood her glance toward Lord Brookes, she turned to Daisy quickly. "I have to talk to him. Cover for me?"

Daisy frowned. "Cover what?"

"My disappearance from the ballroom, for as long as you possibly can. If Bennett asks, tell them I've torn a hem, and it might take a while to have it mended."

"All right." Daisy grabbed her hand and squeezed her fingers. "Good luck."

Gabby glanced down at her hem, winced as if noticing it was damaged, and then hurried from the room, leaving Daisy to explain to her guardian where she'd gone.

Mamble was moving slowly down the hall, and she followed without hesitation. When he slipped into a chamber, she hastened to join him. He stood in what looked like a private study and was entirely alone. Gabby shut the door softly behind her and locked it for good measure.

Mamble's head cocked to one side, clearly hearing her arrival.

Gabby moved toward the duke. "Your grace," she said, but her voice sounded odd to her ears. Husky and breathless and very unlike her own.

"I'm not interested," he drawled. "Go back where you came from, madam."

Gabby was not to be deterred by his instant dismissal. He assumed she was someone else again. She knew just what to say to begin this conversation. "I'm not a maid, my lord, but someone who wishes to say how ardently I admire you."

"Is that so?" He spun around, and his expression of pleasure gave her courage to continue.

"Yes." There was no point in hiding the truth. They were alone together again, and she *was* too bold. But she really liked him, and it was too late to turn back her feelings. "Your grace, I wish to tell you that from the first we met, I have longed to know you better."

There was silence for a long moment, and then he folded his arms across his chest and regarded her sternly. "I believe you said almost the exact same thing about someone else not so long ago."

Gabby nodded. They were recreating their very first conversation. Only this time, she hoped for a far different outcome. "I did, and yes, I knew you were not Lord Brookes when I walked through that door tonight."

"And there are still a thousand reasons why I am grateful to be spared that fate," the Duke of Mamble said, then his eyes narrowed at her. "Are you sure?"

"Yes. You are the only gentleman on my mind," she admitted with a shy smile.

He kept a distance, finger tapping his lips. "You once looked at a man with a title as if he was something to bite into, too."

"I did no such thing," she protested again, fighting a smile. "And the way you stared at me tonight was quite provocative. One would think you want to devour *me*."

He drew closer. "I do. Were you really surprised I would stare at you tonight?" He looked her up and down and then smiled at her in the very same way he had the first time they'd met. He kept undressing her with his eyes, and Gabby enjoyed the sensation of heat his scrutiny provided. "You're a rather tasty morsel, Gabby. I am very tempted to take a bite of you tonight."

Gabby's face blazed hot, as did the rest of her. She understood better now all that it could mean between a man and a woman to talk this way. She easily imagined Mamble's teeth grazing her neck and his kisses making her moan out loud.

She was better prepared for an encounter with him now than she had been at the beginning of their acquaintance. The duke was outrageously bold and knew how to say just the right thing to turn her head and yet he did nothing improper beyond that in public. Underneath all his bluster, he followed the rules of polite society. He had not rushed her into his arms but teased her until she had wanted to be. How could she not have fallen for such a man? "Will you say such things when we're engaged?"

His lips curved into a smile. "I imagine I would. I gather, we are of the same mind about the possibilities between us at last. If you were not, you still have a chance to run. I would understand."

"I don't want to run away from you," she whispered.

His hand rose to cup her face. "I heard you've become my defender, attempting to right the wrong the gossiping hoard have against me. A kitten with claws soon to become a dragon of the *ton*, perhaps."

"I had to say something in your defense. You're not the man they describe," she whispered. "You are good."

"Not always good and neither are you," he warned. His

bare palm was so warm against her cheek that she leaned into his touch. "You followed me for a kiss, didn't you?"

"I followed you because...Yes, I want," she began, and would have said more, except Mamble pressed his thumb over her lips.

"Gabby mine."

Gabby could not stop the smile that burst from her then. Mamble had captured her heart, and she seemed to have caught him, too, though she had not heard him say he loved her.

Lord Mamble's thumb was still pressed against her lips, and before she knew it, her tongue darted out to taste him again.

His eyes flared, and a wicked smile curved his lips. "You need to stop doing that," he whispered as his thumb dragged slowly off her bottom lip. "You'd be shocked by the thoughts that fill my head right now. But I like that in a woman. Boldness and passion."

Gabby lowered her eyes a little. Passion was something she had yet to experience.

He bent until their eyes were on the same level again. Gabby's heart raced as she stared into the duke's knowing blue gaze. She was not afraid of what came next between them. It would be as extraordinary as meeting him. Mamble gently drew her into his arms, holding her close, and breathed deep. "Are you ready now for a wolf like me, Gabby?"

She grinned. "Are you sure you're ready for *me*?"

Chapter Ten

"SHALL WE FIND OUT." Sebastian bent his head and delivered a soft kiss upon her lips, one he hoped earned her trust. With that one kiss he knew why he was drawn to her.

He loved her.

This was no woman he could walk away from. There was no turning back. He'd known it deep in his soul the moment they'd met where he longed to be. By her side, forever. Watching over her as she found her feet in society.

Her response was hesitant at first but then she suddenly wasn't. The kitten became bolder. Matching him in passion, kiss for kiss. Encouraging more by copying him.

When he teased his fingers into her hair, she did the same with him. When he slid his hands down her back to her rear, she copied that too, and they laughed together when their arms became entangled.

Their lives would become entwined now, too. He'd not counted on falling in love this season, but he loved a woman who had never wanted to become his duchess. Yet she would become one as soon as he could negotiate a marriage contract with her guardian, and he couldn't imagine a more deserving woman by his side.

She was kind, smart, and no wilting wallflower. She was already so dear to him. And keen to be his sister's friend. He almost couldn't believe he'd been so lucky.

He drew back to look into her eyes again. "Do you love me?"

"I do, your grace," she promised.

"Remember those two words for later," he whispered, tapping her nose, "And it's Sebastian from now on."

"Sebastian," she whispered, an impish grin on her face. "My Sebastian."

"Yes, my love. I am well and truly caught," he whispered, astonished to see tears fill her eyes at his words.

Sebastian led her to a settee close to the fire and settled her on his lap. Gabby laughed and squirmed, no doubt unused to such things, but he held her close against his chest and breathed a sigh of relief.

He could not bear to let her go yet. But he would have to soon, of course. He must send her back to the ballroom and follow at a discreet distance. He would not have his future duchess' reputation tarnished by scandal before their engagement was even announced.

He pressed his brow to hers. "What changed your mind about me?"

"I don't know that it ever changed," she told him. "I just needed to get to know you, and myself as well. There's more to choosing a husband than picking one at first glance," she warned him.

"What else is there to want from a suitor than a handsome face, wealth and a title?"

"A man with a kind and loving heart. You had no reason to dance with me that first night. But you did, and that one act of kindness changed the course of my life. The way you are with your sister was also endearing. I could see how protective of her you were. I believe in that, and in you."

Overcome with emotion, Sebastian kissed her again and turned her about, pressing her back against the arm of the chaise. He'd known he wanted this woman, desired her, but it had been his soul crying out for her, too.

Gabby wound her arms about his shoulders and kissed him back with so much encouragement that soon he was pulling up her skirts. He stopped himself with a muttered curse and buried his face in the crook of her neck. "My dear, you excite me too much, too easily."

He felt her lips against his ear, and then her teeth nibbled the lobe. "Did I ask you to stop?"

He looked up at her in astonishment. "No."

She smiled. "I am bold, and I want you to touch me in ways I don't fully understand yet. But I'm not afraid of what comes next, Sebastian. Something has to."

Sebastian slid his hand down her side. "It doesn't have to be tonight," he promised.

"Sebastian. My Sebastian," she whispered. "But it will be."

Given he had permission, his fingers continued down her thigh until he found bare flesh. He teased his fingers slowly up to her sex. Gabby's eyes were wide open, and her breath came in little pants as he touched her sex for the first time, gently, reverently, but it was clear she wasn't going to stop him.

She was damp and willing, and Sebastian wanted her so much. He had to at least see her climax tonight. The rest could come during their courtship. He could not imagine waiting until their wedding night to share all that loving her could mean.

He teased his finger along her folds, gently parting her

and exploring carefully. He found her clit as he claimed her mouth in a fierce kiss, swallowing her gasp. He teased his tongue into her depths, even as his finger found her entrance. He carefully teased her there for a while as she squirmed and pushed against his fingers. He could easily tell what he was doing wasn't enough for her. She would climax soon, but not before he got a proper taste.

He indulged in one last heated kiss before he moved down the chaise to put his head between her pale thighs. And when he put his mouth to work beside his fingers, he feared everyone in the ballroom would hear her moans and come running.

He kissed her sex, dragged his tongue along her folds and stabbed into her for his first proper taste. But time was short, and she was a virgin, too, so Sebastian confined himself to that one indulgence.

He found her clitoris again and devoted himself to proving himself as a lover. Kissing her and rubbing the flat of his tongue across her most sensitive parts. It did not take long before Gabby's knees rose to cradle his head, and she climaxed a moment later.

Her grip slowly loosened when she was done, and he quickly rose up over her. She stared up at him with soft, languid eyes, seemingly destroyed by her climax. He dropped a quick kiss to her lips and separated them fully. "We have to get you back to the ballroom."

His erection, though, stuck out painfully hard in his breeches, and he didn't try to hide it from her. She had to know this about him one day soon. When they were married, he imagined they'd spend many hours together, aroused or sated.

She sat up, eyes on his groin, which did not help his condition abate in any way. When she stood, eventually, he did his best to help straighten her gown. She was mussed, unfortunately. He tried to smooth her skirts, but she stilled his hands.

"Don't worry about that now," she said with a smile. "I asked Daisy to tell Bennett that I was having my hem mended. That will explain any added wrinkles."

He looked at Gabby in surprise. "Daisy knew you were coming to me?"

"Yes," Gabby said with a shrug. "She's my friend. I would do the same for her, too."

"I owe her now as well," he promised. He went to the door and glanced outside. "Time for you to go," he whispered to Gabby reluctantly.

"Sebastian? What happens next?"

He noticed her fidgets and closed the door again. "We dance, and tomorrow I call on your guardian to formally ask for your hand in marriage."

"Another dance?" she teased; brow arched high.

"Can you bear it?"

"I long for it," Gabby assured him. "I'll go back to Daisy, and I'll see you there soon."

She slipped out the door, and Sebastian waited a few minutes before following. As he arrived in the ballroom, a hush fell over the gathering.

He slowed his steps, fearing Gabby had somehow given them away. She was standing beside her guardian now. Her face was pale as she clung to his arm.

Sebastian hurried to join them. "What is it?"

"There's been a development," Bennett whispered, eyes locked on the far side of the room.

Across from them were Lord Brookes, Lady Whitlow, and Justine Dawes. And they appeared to be arguing. In public. In a manner that could clearly be heard by everyone near them in the ballroom. A silence descended over everyone else at the gathering.

"You made a promise to me!" Lady Whitlow complained loudly.

Lord Brookes looked around, eyes a little desperate and wild. "Lower your voice."

Lady Whitlow stabbed her finger into his chest. "You said if I did you that favor, you'd marry. Shall I tell everyone what it was you asked of me?"

Lord Brookes turned decidedly pale. "No. I will keep my word."

"Tonight," Lady Whitlow demanded, her eyes triumphant.

Sebastian winced. Lord Brookes looked to have trapped himself into making a marriage. Finally, one of the ladies he'd led on would bring him up to scratch.

As Sebastian looked across the room, he couldn't help but notice that Justine Dawes had turned pale as Lord Brookes took up her sister's hand.

He glanced at Gabby, wondering what she thought of this turn of events.

"This is terrible. Poor Justine," Gabby whispered. "Such a scandal."

Although Gabby had whispered the question to him, Justine shot her a look of pure venom. Gabby flinched, and Sebastian moved closer to her side.

She looked up at him. "Why is she doing this in front of everyone?"

"To force his hand," he told her, even as Brookes was lowering himself to one knee before Lady Whitlow. No one paid attention to the sister's dismayed expression.

Sebastian turned away. He'd seen enough.

"I could never have done that just to become a wife."

"There will never be a need. Lady Whitlow got what she wanted, and in the same manner as she acquired her first husband. She's fond of a match under the threat of blackmail," Sebastian murmured.

Justine moved to stand behind the pair, her eyes lowered now.

People started moving around and whispering as the prospective bride and future groom were encouraged to dance together. To celebrate their match, such as it was.

Sebastian vowed that at the next ball, society would celebrate a better-made match. One both parties wanted.

He turned to Gabby and held out his hand. "May I have the pleasure of the next dance, Miss Kimble?"

"I would be deeply honored, your grace," she said immediately, throwing him a shy smile.

Sebastian reached for his hand.

As they took the floor, along with others, he glanced at Justine Dawes one last time. She stood alone and continued to regard the floor. He felt pity for her. She'd made a mistake turning her back on true friends.

His glance darted across the room to where Lord Brookes had just clumsily trod on his future bride's foot. Lady Whitlow limped to the sidelines, but Brookes turned the other way, leaving her to her friends. There had never been a more ill matched couple in his entire memory. Yet Brookes had proved himself an enemy. He had tried to blacken his character to Gabby's guardian. Sebastian could not forgive him for that.

Sebastian drew Gabby into his arms a little tighter and let out a sigh. "It's the ultimate revenge."

"What is?"

"Our engagement."

Gabby glanced up at him and frowned. "I could never see it that way."

"That warms my heart to hear," he promised as they spun about the floor together, perfectly in tune with each other.

Epilogue

Gabby sat impatiently in her new bedchamber, her fingers playing with the delicate fabric of her wedding gown. It was the day of her nuptials, and she was about to marry the man of her dreams.

She couldn't believe how lucky she was and how deeply she adored her future husband. Four months of courtship, longing glances, and a few precious, stolen hours where they had been completely alone with each other.

Gabby had lost her innocence to Sebastian the night their wedding date had been announced, and Sebastian had been the most attentive suitor ever since.

Tonight, they would be alone together all night long, and she could not wait. She would have Sebastian naked in his bed or in hers. And tomorrow, his would be the first face she saw.

As she waited for Bennett to come and fetch her to give her away, her mind wandered back to the day when she first met Sebastian. He'd affected her from the start, but she had not realized what their relationship might become until many weeks had passed.

And now, they would be husband and wife. It was to be a small, private ceremony in his home, with only their closest friends and family in attendance. Cordelia had organized everything for their special day. Lady Windermere had provided Gabby's wedding gown, a trousseau, and information about how she might satisfy her husband and herself in their marriage bed.

Gabby had blushed through those entire conversations, because there were so many ways to pleasure a man or woman when they loved each other.

"I can't wait to be a bride," Daisy said as she stood before the mirror in Gabby's new room, admiring her reflection in the full-length mirror.

"To anyone in particular?" Gabby asked, throwing her a teasing smile. "Or just anyone brave enough to take you on?"

"I'm still hopeful for a love match like yours and Mamble's," Daisy said with a heavy sigh.

Daisy was sweet and gentle on the surface, but she had developed a bit of a temper, especially when her guardian kept getting in her way. She needed just the right man to sweep her off her feet and out from under Lord Throsby's thumb. It was either that or wait for Daisy to reach her majority in a few weeks and find her future husband without his interference.

Bennett appeared at the door at last. "It's time."

"Yes," Gabby agreed, standing up and heading for the door. "My future is waiting."

Bennett bowed. "Yes, duchess."

She frowned at him and then kissed his cheek. "I'm still Gabby to you, dear cousin."

"Still my responsibility for a few more minutes, too," he noted. He glanced at Daisy. "Would you mind giving us a moment, please?"

"Of course. I'll wait outside the drawing room doors for you both," Daisy said before rushing off downstairs.

Gabby looked at Bennett. "Is something wrong with your room?"

"No. The room here is perfect," he promised, but then winced. "But I fear I cannot stay here much longer."

"I see no reason for you to leave," Gabby said, grabbing his arm. "After all you've done for me over the years, bringing me to London and being so understanding about Sebastian. I want you to stay with us. *We* want you to live here with us."

"I'll only be in the way," he said. "I've already discussed the matter with Sebastian, and he understands my misgivings. You are newlyweds and need time alone. You'll barely notice I'm gone."

Gabby gripped his arm a little tighter. "Is this about Cordelia?"

"It's about me," he promised. "But I think you haven't heard that Lady Cordelia will be returning to the countryside, too, this afternoon. I'm so proud of you, Gabby. Your mother and father would be so proud of you as well. They never imagined this could be your future, but it's time for me to live my own life again. I'm going home."

Gabby's eyes filled with tears. "No."

Home was a world away from Gabby's new life as a duchess.

"It's time," he assured her with a soft smile. "You don't need me to boss around anymore. You have Mamble for that."

"But who will look after you?"

"I'll have you know I did a passably good job looking after myself before you landed on my doorstep. I'll be fine, Gabby," he promised, tugging her toward the stairs. "But if it eases your mind, I put notices in the paper for a housekeeper last week, and I've already found a good one. She comes highly recommended by Lady Windermere herself."

"Well, that is a weight off my mind, but I still don't want you to go, or Cordelia. Promise you'll reconsider or come back for a visit soon," she begged. "You must write."

"I promise I will," he told her, and then marched her down the stairs of Mamble House. "Though I know your letters will be far more exciting than mine could ever be."

"I don't know about that. I still want to know about you and what you're doing and who you meet. The first thing of course is to tell me all about your new housekeeper. I expect a full description of the woman."

"I will," he promised with a smile, but by then they had reached the drawing room doors.

Daisy handed her a posy of wildflowers and nodded. "He's waiting for you."

Gabby bit her lip. "Is she here?"

Daisy shook her head quickly. "I wouldn't think Justine would dare show her face after the rude way she treated you. She's not been seen very much at all since Lord Brookes married her sister. I do believe she's been thoroughly put in her place. Still, such a betrayal turns ones stomach. However, choosing ambition over friendship never turns out well for anyone."

"I had hoped she might still come..." she started but then shrugged.

"She chose this path when she continued to snub you after your engagement was announced," Bennett whispered as he nudged her. "Some people just cannot be happy for others. The best revenge you can have over such a person is to live happily ever after. You chose well. You chose love. Mamble just happens to come with a tiny insignificant title. You will make a remarkable duchess."

"Thank you."

Gabby squared her shoulders and grinned. It was time for a great many changes. First of which would be her name to make that dream come true of marrying for love. She marched through the drawing room doors on her guardian's arm for the last time as his ward, she smiled thinking of the other plans set in motion for him later.

But for now, her only thought was for the most handsome, beguiling devil that she could love to distraction forever.

Bennett Kimble stumbled from the saddle and led his horse into its usual stall in the stables, stretching out the kinks from his back as he went. It had been a long journey, and he was worn out and ready for his bed and a good night's sleep.

He headed for his modest little cottage nestled on the border of the grand Scarsdale estate. It was good to be home, but he expected to notice the quiet for a long time. However, he would need to make a call there tomorrow most likely and share the news of Gabby's marriage to a duke last week. Then there would be his patients to call on, ailments to tend. He imagined he'd have a very busy month ahead.

Not that he regretted the time he'd been gone. Going back had opened his eyes to what he had here and what was still impossible. The stability and contentment of the countryside might not suit everyone, but it suited him. Here there were no temptations and in London there had been plenty to choose from but only one he'd wanted but had to deny himself.

He paused as he noticed smoke rose from the kitchen chimney straight up toward the heavens which meant his new housekeeper had already have arrived to take up her new position.

He was anxious to meet the woman he'd hired without meeting first and wished he could keep her name in mind. But his cousin, Lady Windermere, had deemed the woman suitable to run his small household and he'd gone along with hiring her sight unseen. But time would tell if they could get along together. There was very little she would need to actually do which might just send her packing for a better position somewhere else.

He removed his hat as he stepped through the front door and as he hung it on its customary peg, he heard footsteps and humming coming from the rear of building. A musical housekeeper. It felt disloyal to Gabby to be relieved about that. Gabby hadn't had much musical talent, no matter how hard or long she'd practiced.

"I'm home," he called out.

The humming stopped and footsteps rushed about but did not come closer.

Puzzled that there was no response, he headed toward the sounds.

The new housekeeper was in the morning room at the hearth, copper kettle in hand, mop cap on her head hiding the color of her hair and her features.

He cleared his throat and the woman stood and turned.

Bennett couldn't speak for a full minute as he stared at the *lady*.

"Cordelia? What are you doing here?"

"Making you a cup of tea. You must be tired after your journey from London." She quickly filled the pot on the table as if waiting on him was a perfectly ordinary thing for her to do. She glanced his way and smiled. "Like you, I decided my brother's marriage was the perfect time to run away from society. I just never knew where to go. Gabby happily supplied your address and Lady Windermere offered her carriage for my journey. Do you mind seeing me again?"

Bennett's legs buckled and he folded into a chair. "He'll mind. The duke, I mean."

"Nonsense." She set a teapot on the table and then a plate of freshly made biscuits. She drew closer and her hand landed on his shoulder. After a moment it drifted up and her fingers stroked his cheek. "Everyone told him I needed doctoring."

Bennett burst to his feet, catching hold of her fingers. "None of that nonsense with me. Fine acting on your part though. You have society convinced you're the mad young lady from that last play we performed in together and made yourself unfit for marriage in the process. You only needed..."

He gulped.

Cordelia smiled and looped her arms about his neck, laying her body against his. "I need the man that fell in love with me years ago to rescue me from a fate worse than death. A loveless match based solely on my huge dowry. I had to do something to thwart my family. You broke my heart, disappeared from London so suddenly without leaving me a crumb of hope. Gabby told me why you left but at the time I never knew where you'd gone until I saw you again standing in the morning room and looking so shocked to see me again."

"I didn't know what to say in front of your brother. You were so far out of my reach still."

"Well, I am very much in your reach now, sir," she whispered. "I thought I'd never see you again, Bennett."

Bennett set his hands lightly on her waist and a slow grin broke free of his control. "I feared that, too. I only learned later your father had banished you to the countryside. I expected you to be married off to some rich noble."

"It never went so far as that. There was no proposal to refuse. I called upon my acting skills to save me from such a match. My father died thinking I was mad and by then I was happy to avoid society entirely. Poor Sebastian. I fear I might have worried him unnecessarily, but I could not take the risk of being matched with anyone else. Not when I still loved you."

"What am I going to do with you, Cordie?"

"Marry me."

Bennett reached up and tugged the cap from her head, releasing a spill of liquid gold strands that tumbled halfway down her back. He backed her toward the nearest wall. He had first met Cordelia at the theatre and instantly fallen in love. But he was a nobody. Never good enough to marry a duke's daughter. Yet Cordelia had taken risks to meet with him in secret and still was by following him home. How could he not love her more. "I'd love nothing more than to spend my life with you, but I will absolutely put my foot down. There will be no acting out death scenes in this house."

Cordelia laughed softly. "Of course not, Bennett. There are plenty of other plays we can perform together where there is only happiness by the end."

"Good." He laughed, too. "Now we had better write your brother and inform him of our intentions to marry. I'm sure he'd like the chance to give you away."

"Anything you say Bennett," she promised, "so long as it's a small country wedding. Just us."

He grinned, liking that idea. "That sounds perfect, just as you have always been in my eyes."

Turn the page for a sneak peek at Miss Ellis Unleashed, Book 2 in the Entangled Series

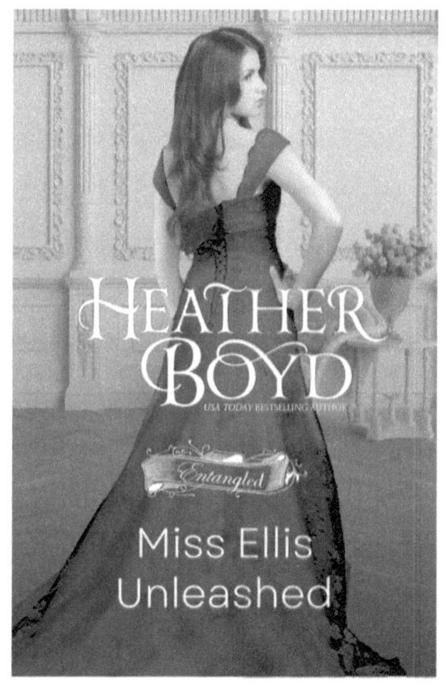

ENTANGLED
Book 2

CHAPTER ONE

Daisy Ellis flinched as the front door of her Golden Square home slammed shut. She gritted her teeth as heavy male footsteps disturbed her peaceful morning yet again. Her guardian, Lord Throsby—an irritable viscount—rushed past the sitting room doorway before his steps faded away toward the rear of the house.

Another door slammed shut, and all fell silent again.

The housekeeper, Mrs. Lamb, quietly set aside her sewing and rose from her nearby chair. "Lord Throsby is back earlier than usual," she murmured, eyes on the door to the hall. She primped her hair absently. "I'd best see if he needs anything."

Daisy rolled her eyes. Her friend Gabby, the Duchess of Mamble, sighed softly as the housekeeper slipped from the room.

Even though the housekeeper was a decade and older than Throsby, Mrs. Lamb had developed a rather transparent soft spot for the surly viscount.

Daisy remained at the table, refusing to become interested in his activities. "No doubt he will think of something she can do for him. Throsby is nothing if not predictable," she said to her esteemed guest.

Gabby smothered a laugh. "Indeed he is."

"He will charge about, call for his valet, change his clothes but depart the house within twenty minutes, ten if we are extremely fortunate," Daisy confessed in a whisper.

"That is how my Sebastian is. Rush, rush, all the time, but every now and then he stops to linger at my side."

"I should hope so," Daisy answered. "A wife is worth lingering over, especially when they are as lovely as you."

Gabby's cheeks turned pink with a blush. She and the

duke were a passionate couple, madly in love, and the duke was not ashamed to prove his interest, no matter where the couple found themselves.

Daisy might have enjoyed a similar devotion, had the viscount gotten out of her way.

She *wished* her stuffy guardian would leave her side. She and Throsby had never gotten along. But everyone else, from the housekeeper down to the boot boy, seemed to tolerate his presence.

Daisy could not understand why.

The man was a menace to her peace.

Before he went out again today, he would poke his stern face through the sitting room doorway and look about the space for any signs of wickedness she might be involved in. He'd demand to know what she'd been doing all morning, as if she could not help but get into great mischief during his brief absences. It was hardly likely she'd have been properly seduced with her best friend in the room—a servant, too—or when he had been gone barely half an hour.

Daisy picked up the news sheet lying neglected on the table and shook it out. Though she was almost too excited to sit still, and certainly there was nothing of consequence in it to warrant a second perusal, she started to read the paper out loud to Gabby.

Daisy had spent the last half hour discussing the fun she would have tonight. But it was the promise of *tomorrow* that occupied her thoughts even more.

Tomorrow would be Daisy's first day as an independent woman. The guardianship she'd chafed under for four years ended tonight at the stroke of midnight.

Daisy had nothing special planned to celebrate her

twentieth birthday other than doing as she pleased at last. After tonight, Throsby would have no power to complain if she misbehaved anymore.

And by misbehaving, she meant simply laughing and having a jolly good time.

She poured another cup of tea for Gabby and topped up her own cup too, smiling to herself, and then continued to recite the paper as her guardian's footsteps inevitably sounded through the house once more.

Throsby rushed everywhere. Inside the house—but never upstairs, thankfully—and out in society, too. Daisy's head spun some nights at the speed in which he made her circle the ballrooms at the entertainments he decided she must attend.

Today, he must have paused only a few minutes to change into fresh clothing. He must be late for an appointment or something equally dull, not that she cared enough to inquire what he was up to.

She preferred to know little about her guardian, especially since he hardly expressed an interest in her opinion. The only kindness he'd ever shown her was allowing Daisy to mourn her father in private before finally bringing her out at nineteen years of age. A little later than most debutants perhaps, but she hadn't been ready to make merry before that.

The season had been fun so far, making new friends, and, in the beginning, her interest in gentlemen and finding a husband had been genuine. But the gentlemen she admired were often not the marrying kind. She accepted that her smaller dowry made her less interesting as a potential bride, and her disinterest in men who valued money over love had grown in leaps and bounds.

Daisy still liked to look at handsome men, to admire them, and to imagine the advantages of choosing one man over the other for her husband.

Unfortunately, once many fellows opened their mouths, beyond pleasantries, she discovered only self-absorbed scoundrels who cared nothing for hearing her opinion, or any other woman's, for that matter. The best men were often already married, like her friend Gabby's husband, Sebastian, Duke of Mamble.

Now, *there* was a man who appreciated an intelligent woman.

Throsby had managed to chase away those who were left, glowering like the beast he had always been because they did not meet with *his* approval.

As if summoned by her thought, the viscount burst into the room without knocking, but after four years, Daisy was prepared for such interruptions. She did not look up and complain about his lack of manners. A true gentleman would have knocked, but her guardian deemed himself above such things. Besides, what would be the point of complaining now? It was the last day he could ever attempt to catch her ignoring the rules of proper society with a suitor who had slipped past his guard.

He sputtered, caught by surprise by the presence of a duchess at Daisy's side. "Oh, forgive me, your grace, I was not informed you were visiting."

Gabby stood. "I was just on my way home again, Lord Throsby. Until tomorrow, Daisy."

Daisy sighed, disappointed that Gabby's visit was to be shorter than her last.

She said goodbye to her friend and watched her waltz out of the room. Daisy resumed her interest in the paper as if the viscount wasn't there.

"I did not mean to interrupt," he murmured.

"Think nothing of it," Daisy answered in an offhand way meant to convey that he surely had.

He cleared his throat loudly to get her attention. "Any other callers of note today?"

She cocked her head to the side, annoyed by the question that surely had to be about potential suitors, and turned the page. "The king called to ask for my hand in marriage. Gabby thinks I should accept."

Throsby scoffed. "The king is already married and not presently in London. You both know that."

Throsby's sense of humor had always been deficient. She closed her eyes and easily imagined his expression right now. He would be wearing a scowl. He always did. Just as he always wore a pristine white shirt, and a navy-blue coat and waistcoat over fawn breeches at this time of day.

His face would be clean-shaven, his hair cut too short, and a plain pocket watch and chain would be draped just above his waist. Understated, night and day. That was her guardian. The man did nothing to draw attention to himself. He was the sort of man women barely looked at twice.

Throsby cleared his throat again. "Will you ever be done with that paper?"

"I assure you I am reading as fast as I can," she promised him.

"With your eyes closed?"

Daisy glanced up at him. Yes, he was exactly as she'd imagined. The man never changed. Throsby was positively glowering at her, too, and Daisy's satisfaction in the day increased to see that reaction. She rather enjoyed upsetting Throsby morning noon and night.

She smiled slowly but out of habit rather than fondness for the viscount looming over her. "They were not closed. I was concentrating."

Throsby snorted but did not call her a liar outright. He was undoubtedly thinking it, though.

Over the years of the guardianship, Daisy had developed a remarkable desire to annoy this man and had discovered what irritated him most of all was a lack of interest in complying with his demands.

Appearing to take all day to read the news sheet was just one of a number she routinely employed to irk him. She took great delight in unsettling him with her other quiet rebellions, too. The best was adjusting her garter in front of him and flashing her stocking-covered ankle. She reserved that for dire emergencies, when she wanted Throsby to leave the house in a tearing hurry.

The viscount appeared easily flustered by a glimpse of stocking, especially hers.

Daisy returned to reading the paper again, but she was aware of the viscount's lingering presence, his huff of annoyance, and his tight grip on the door handle.

The man needed a woman to rid him of all that pent-up tension.

But Throsby had never courted anyone while he'd been her guardian, even when she had conspired to throw a lonely widow directly into his path. The man had stuck to her side like glue for the whole of the season so far, too. But that was all about to end tonight.

She wanted to laugh and shout out her impatience for that moment to come.

Instead, she exhaled softly. "Did you want something else from me, my lord?" She asked the question innocently enough...but she glanced up at him from beneath her lashes while simultaneously leaning down to check if her garter needed adjustment.

The viscount clenched his jaw and resolutely refused to look at what she was doing to her leg. "I'm to meet the Duke of Mamble today at the club for luncheon."

"Yes, Gabby told me all about it. And it's a Tuesday, so you always go out today."

"There was something I wanted to show him from today's paper," he grumbled.

"But I'm not done with reading it yet," she protested, eyes wide with feigned surprise. "What a shame you denied me my own copy so you have to share yours."

She said it mildly enough but inside, she was still seething mad at him for never letting her have her own. He claimed the expense was excessive when they could share.

"Never mind the paper now," he said, sighing heavily afterward. "I'll purchase another copy on my way there."

Daisy shrugged. "Well, good, and have a jolly good time out with your friends."

"The Mambles are your friends, not mine." Throsby's lips thinned briefly, but when Daisy inched her gown up again, he shook his head. "I will return in plenty of time to escort you to tonight's masquerade."

"It will never be said that you have shirked your duty as a guardian, my lord," she murmured, picking up the paper again but stealing a glance at his face first. There was no indication of anticipation for their last ball together or for escorting her there. Yet, he was hesitating to leave. Would she have to throw her gown up over her knees today to drive him away?

Daisy had always assumed Throsby was as eager as herself for an end to their annoying and unnecessary arrangement, but lately, he seemed to linger around as if she needed constant supervision.

Daisy had lost her papa at sixteen years old but had managed the household and her papa's finances for many years before that. She'd hardly needed a guardian to manage so small a sum of money, and certainly not a man like Throsby. He'd been a complete stranger when he had arrived and had taken over everything, despite her protests that she was more than capable and she did not need him.

And it continued to irk her that her papa had saddled her with a humorless lump of a man. Papa's final act as a father had been hard to reconcile.

She squinted at the paper and mumbled a few sentences softly, pretending she didn't fully comprehend what she read, since that too would irk him.

Throsby snorted again. "So, I will be waiting for you at eight o'clock in the hall," he announced as the housekeeper slipped into the room around him.

"Yes, and I will be ready and on time as you expect me to be," she answered, knowing some sort of response was required to complete what had become their daily ritual.

When she said nothing more, he left the room as

abruptly as he'd come, and the front door slammed shut behind him.

Daisy tossed the paper aside in disgust and looked around the cluttered room.

Just a few more hours and then...freedom.

Her home would be her own again, she could spread out her belongings, and her servants would take *her* orders and not his. And she would have the distinct pleasure of having *her* servants move her father's old bed back upstairs to the currently empty master chamber where it should have remained all along.

There would be no more pleasing Lord Throsby's needs under this roof.

Daisy sighed as the housekeeper sat at her side once more.

Some supervision *was* required from time to time, though. She wasn't completely immoral.

"You can come out now, Mr. Pinkerton," Daisy called, and then flipped up the long cloth covering the table and peeked under. "He'll be gone for five and forty minutes at the very least.

"I thought he'd never leave," Pinkerton replied, as he emerged from under the table. He straightened his coat, smoothed his hair, and cast a cheeky smile toward the housekeeper. "That was close. I was certain he'd find me this time."

To continue reading visit:
https://heather-boyd.com/miss-ellis-unleashed

WILD RANDALLS SERIES

Engaging the Enemy ~ Forsaking the Prize

Guarding the Spoils ~ Hunting the Hero

*

SAINTS AND SINNERS SERIES

The Duke and I ~ A Gentleman's Vow

An Earl of Her Own ~ The Lady Tamed

*

REBEL HEARTS SERIES

The Wedding Affair ~ An Affair of Honor

The Christmas Affair ~ An Affair so Right

*

MISS MAYHEM SERIES

Miss Watson's First Scandal

Miss George's Second Chance

Miss Radley's Third Dare

Miss Merton's Last Hope

About Heather Boyd

USA Today Bestselling Author Heather Boyd believes every character she creates deserves their own happily-ever-after—no matter how much trouble she puts them through. With that goal in mind, she writes steamy romances that skirt the boundaries of propriety to keep readers enthralled until the wee hours of the morning. Heather has published over sixty regency romance novels and shorter works full of daring seductions and distinguished rogues. She lives north of Sydney, Australia, with her trio of rogues and a four-legged overlord.

Find out more about Heather at:
Heather-Boyd.com

facebook.com/HeatherBoydRomanceAuthor

instagram.com/heatherboydbooks

bookbub.com/authors/heather-boyd

goodreads.com/Heather_Boyd

9 781922 733450